EXODUS INTO EVIL

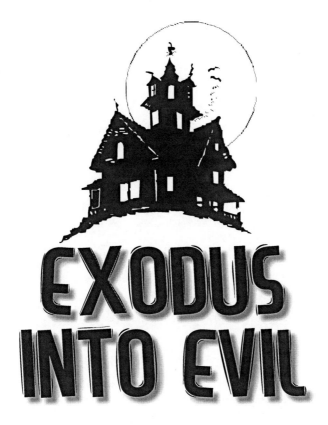

EXODUS INTO EVIL

A Collection of Short Horror Stories

STANLEY J. BRZYCKI

iUniverse, Inc.
Bloomington

EXODUS INTO EVIL
A COLLECTION OF SHORT HORROR STORIES

iUniverse books may be ordered through booksellers or by contacting:

iUniverse
1663 Liberty Drive
Bloomington, IN 47403
www.iuniverse.com
1-800-Authors (1-800-288-4677)

ISBN: 978-1-4620-5443-5 (sc)
ISBN: 978-1-4620-5445-9 (hc)
ISBN: 978-1-4620-5444-2 (ebk)

Printed in the United States of America

iUniverse rev. date: 12/06/2011

Το my parents, brother, and sisters, who taught me to be devious, determined, and to never give up on my goals. To Linda Wenrick, who gave me my first Stephen King book. To Linda Fulop and Geoff Vanderbeck, who inspired the stories "The Chair" and "The Unknown Factor". For Susan Songer (The Saddle Lady): my special friend, beautiful, outspoken, talented, and much more, I'm thankful every day for knowing you. And to Stephen King, whose book *On Writing* inspired me to write my first book at the youthful age of fifty!

WHO AM I?

I love driving along Highway 22 east of Salem. I was headed for a small town called Detroit, Oregon, on a bright, sunny day with all the uncertainty I had ever felt in my life. My name is Mark, and I'm a writer of short stories. I was hoping that the proper inspiration for my first book could be found in the town of Detroit. My home had been Portland, Oregon, for most of my life. I'd been able to generate a good living with my short stories, but I was ready for the next step, a novel good enough so that I could be recognized as an accomplished writer. My parents had a cottage in the town of Detroit and had given it to me before they died last year. I hadn't been to the cottage for years, so I didn't know what to expect. As I pulled into the town, I noticed I needed gas, so I drove into a gas station and was surprised to find a familiar face pumping gas. It was Ed Munson, a childhood fishing friend from when my mom and dad had brought me up here.

"Good grief. Hi, Eddie, how are you, man?"

"Mark, is that you? Jeez, you look good. Are you still writing those stories?"

"Yeah, making a living at it, sort of."

We both laughed hard.

"What brings you up here, Mark?"

"Well, I'm going to try and write my first book, but right now I could use some gas."

"Sure thing, Mark. Let me know if you want to get together, okay?"

"Sure thing, Eddie."

After filling up, I drove my '66 Mustang Fastback to the cottage to settle in. Upon arrival I realized the cottage was in need of a good cleaning, but other than that it felt like a warm place and drew me in with its charm. I emptied my little trailer of all it's belongings and did some looking through the remaining items for items I had forgotten. By early evening I was all settled in. The hairs on my neck stiffened and rose at a strange odor in the air. It was familiar and dangerous! The moist ground concealed my footsteps as I traveled along the path I knew so well. I stayed out of the moonlight for safety.

Mark woke up and rolled over. His head pounded dully as he opened his bloodshot eyes. *God, I hate mornings!* he thought to himself. Looking at his clock, he realized there wasn't much morning left, about two hours.

Mark thought that he should get up just so he could say he got up this morning, instead of this afternoon, which would have been more to his liking. If he did get those extra few hours of sleep, he might have gotten rid of those weird dreams he'd been having. He moved through the cottage, as if on autopilot, made a bathroom stop (but did not shower—it was his grunge, casual day), and headed for the kitchen. He gave the legal pads a passing glance and the computer a disgusted revolting stare. Mark had always written his stories in longhand on legal pads. For some reason he had a block against writing on a computer; it seemed less personal.

Mark had come up here a few times whenever he was having a tough time writing one of his short stories; it seemed easier to be creative here. Glancing in the fridge, he tried to decide on something to eat. It wasn't so much what to eat as how energetic he was about making breakfast; a big breakfast of eggs, hash browns, and bacon sounded good, or perhaps just a bowl of cereal?

Cereal seemed to fit his casual mood. He sat on his sofa and watched a Perry Mason episode that he never got tired of. At the commercial break, he glanced at his bookcase to the right of his TV. It was a modest five-shelf model about six feet long, and it held mostly two authors: Dean Koontz and his favorite, Stephen King. Mark had read all of King's works and had over half in first-edition hardbacks. Mark secretly hoped to be as good as King one day. Time went by, and the TV droned on. When Mark chose to write, it was like a living force within him needing to come out, with the massaging firmness of a guiding caressing hand.

Mark worked—if it could be called that—for about six hours, shaping words to bring out his ideas. Writing was more of a passion than work. Mark always felt so satisfied when he completed a project. Living by himself, Mark hadn't done much dating since the death of his first wife. He wouldn't have survived had it not been for his writing.

I look through these eyes, and my instincts cause me to shudder with rage. All I am doing is looking toward a forest shrouded in night, the night sounds reaching my ears. The air smells so good, full of the smells of damp earth and fir trees. Slowly I walk along the forest edge. Something is watching me. I feel it. It is cold tonight. My breath can be seen in long white plumes as I exhale. Suddenly I hear a faint noise. My ears prick up, trying to locate a direction of the sound. I head off down the path that leads to a pond I know. As I near the pond, I peer out from the trees. In the moonlight I see a deer standing at the pond edge, drinking quietly. I become aware that I'm drooling. I leap from the cover of the trees, moving the ten feet between me and the deer in two leaps, and landing on the deer's neck. As she goes down, her head underwater, I'm not sure if she drowns or if I broke her neck, but she lies still as I drag her behind the trees and feast. Afterward I wash my face in the pond and vocally let all the other animals know that I am hunting this night.

Mark decided to take a break and go for a walk to the pond. It always helped relax him and clear his mind. As he came around the cottage he noticed one of the screens over the window was popped out. After putting it back in he moved down to the pond and noticed two sets of very large footprints in the muddy trail, the biggest he had ever seen. He was beginning to wonder if being outside was such a good idea. The forest was as still as could be until a voice behind him said, "Hi," scaring Mark and making him jump.

"Sorry, I didn't mean to startle you. My name is Mike."

"Boy, did you make me jump. My name is Mark. I came to the pond to relax but got worried when I saw those huge footprints near my home."

3

"Well, I'm prepared if anything jumps out at us here," said Mike as he lifted his rifle. "Mark, there is a fresh kill, or what's left of it, behind the trees. I live just down this other path, if you ever need anything. By the way, Mark, are you the writer that I've heard about?"

"Yeah, I'm the one. How did you know?"

"Eddie at the gas station likes to talk a lot."

Both Mike and Mark laughed out loud at that and then headed home. But Mark's curiosity got the better of him and he had to take a look at the animal kill. After all, how bad could it be? As Mark looked behind the trees he almost vomited. The sight of the kill and the smell were vile. The animal had been torn apart, with only shreds of the pelt left to identify it as a large doe. What could do this type of savagery?

The next afternoon Mark had a visitor. Mike stopped by.

"Hi, Mike."

"Hi, Mark. Could I come in for a moment to talk with you?"

"Sure, Mike. Want a beer?"

"Sure."

As Mark got their beers, Mike started telling him some hunting stories his father and grandfather had passed down over the campfires.

"Mark, I think I saw one of the animals my dad used to tell me about last night at dusk. It was huge—at least two hundred pounds—and black as coal and crossed a corner of my yard."

"Maybe it was a bear."

"No, wrong shape. Too streamlined, and it moved very fast, not cumbersome like a bear."

"What do you think it was?"

"A wolf!"

"Mike, wolves of that size are extinct now. It couldn't have been a wolf."

"That's what I thought until last night, but we'll see what happens in the near future."

Mike finished his beer and shook Mark's hand, thanking him for listening, and left.

Moving through the woods, I heard the sounds of danger: loud laughing, music, and other stupid sounds. I growled low in my throat. Suddenly, the men on the cabin stoop yelled at me and shot at me, saying they could see my yellow eyes. They missed with their shots,

 4

and I retreated, thinking that I would return one day so they could get a good up-close look at my eyes and my contempt for them as I ripped out their throats. Then who would be laughing?

Mark decided he needed to go to his doctor in Salem. His dreams kept coming. He had memory lapses, sore muscles, a temperature, and scratches he couldn't account for. The doctor prescribed him a mild sedative to sleep better and to get more rest. The doctor also recommended checking with the paramedic rescue unit that helped him when he crashed his car previously, to see if anything unusual happened.

Mark was in luck. The rescue unit that helped him out of his car in the crash was ten minutes away, and the paramedic was on duty. Jim King greeted Mark with a hand shake as Mark thanked him for helping him again.

"My pleasure, Mark. Is there anything else I can help you with?"

"Well, Jim, this might sound like a weird question, but did you or the others notice anything unusual happening around the accident site as you came down to get me?"

"To be honest, Mark, we did notice something, but we dismissed it as the light playing tricks on us."

"What was it, Jim?"

"We thought we saw a large animal next to you as you hung outside your car door, but when we got down to you there was nothing there. If there was an animal, it had to be at least two hundred pounds, maybe more."

"Thanks, Jim, for the information."

"I hope it eases your mind. Take care."

I saw your cabin and heard your drunken laughter. I promised to return and I did. I waited till it quieted down, creeping quietly out of the woods. I couldn't wait. I lunged at the window and crashed it, my body barely squeezing inside the stinking cabin. Three men were there. The first grabbed at his rifle, screaming as I snarled and ripped his throat out. I pounced on the other two at the same time. They struggled under the weight of my body, seeing only my black fur and bloodshot yellow eyes. The last thing they saw was a shower of red from their bodies as I took my sweet revenge. As I left, a man came out of a little house near the cabin with one funny door and a cresent moon cut out of it at the top. I jumped him before he could yell and slammed him to the ground, hearing a loud snap as he lay still, eyes unblinking. It was a good night. I pranced into the forest, swiftly looking for food. I refused to eat these humans I killed. They stunk; eating a skunk would have been more satisfying.

Mark was doing chores around the cottage when he noticed a travel trailer pull up next door. A lady got out with moving people and started unloading. The woman was pretty, and she seemed strong lifting heavy items along with the movers. After the move, Mark waved to her and asked if she would like a cold beer. She smiled and said, "Sure." As Mark took the beers over, he introduced himself.

"Hi, my name's Mark," he said, handing her a beer.

"Hi, Mark, my name's Clara, and thanks a lot." She took a long drink from the bottle. "That really hits the spot."

"Have you been to Detroit before?" Mark asked.

"Yes, my father still lives here, and the cottage I'm moving into just went up for sale so I bought it to be near family."

By this time it was around five, Mark decided to be forward. "Clara, do you hate cooking as much as I do when I'm tired?"

"I sure do. Did you have something in mind?"

"Well, would you like to go to the local café and grab some dinner? It's close enough to walk if you like."

"That would be great. I love walking and the outdoors."

So they took off after changing into clothes that weren't so sweat stained. Clara surprised Mark by linking her arm in his, which made him blush as they walked. Clara noticed.

"Mark, don't tell me you're shy."

"Oh no, I'm not shy. It's just been a while since a beautiful woman took my arm like that."

"Good, I was hoping you weren't shy, and thank you for the sweet words."

Mark could not believe it. Here he was, walking a beautiful woman to dinner after just meeting her as she hugged his arm tenderly; it was like winning the lottery.

After Mark and Clara finished dinner they walked back to Clara's home. It had been a great night, but before Mark could say good night, Clara leaned into him and kissed him slowly on the lips.

"I don't remember when I've had such a nice time out, Mark."

"Do you think you would like to get together again, Clara?"

"Yes, do you like picnics?"

"Sure."

"Let's have a picnic tomorrow, okay?"

"That would be great."

This time Mark pulled Clara firmly against his body, put his arms around her, and kissed her deeply. Mark watched as Clara went inside the French doors of her cottage. When Mark got home he couldn't remember walking up the path. All he remembered was kissing Clara!

The next day Mark went over to Clara's home for their picnic. Clara asked him in, as she was almost ready. Mark noticed a lot of long white and gray hairs around her home but no pets. Clara drove her truck with Mark to the special picnic spot. Mark had to admit that it was beautiful—a large pasture with grass and a stream flowing through it at the base of a forested hilltop. After they set out a blanket and ate, they lay in the sun talking.

"Mark, what do you think about going for a swim?"

"We don't have any suits."

"Haven't you ever been skinny-dipping?"

With that they both started laughing and raced each other to the stream as they took their clothes off and dove in. They both started splashing and playing in the water, goofing around. Then Clara came close to Mark and they held each other for a long time, kissing and touching each other.

"Oh, Mark, you're so wonderful."

"So are you, Clara!"

Mark and Clara spent the rest of the day making love and knowing each other in every way a man and woman can possibly know one another. Little did they know that a pair of eyes was watching them from the forested hilltop.

I didn't think she would bring him to the pasture so soon. With that, the large gray wolf lay down, crossed his paws, and went to sleep deeply.

Today was so sunny as I walked the banks of the large stream. A noise drew me; it was a fisherman lying down and getting a nap stream-side. He snored loudly as I crept up on him. I leaped and landed my full weight on his chest, waking him up and knocking the air from him so he couldn't scream. All he saw as he looked into my deep yellow eyes was anger, and I grabbed his head in my jaws and crushed it.

Mike was in town later in the day and saw some activity at the police station. He decided to stop by and talk to a friend, who informed Mike that some hunters and a fisherman had been attacked. It looked almost like they had been butchered. Mike walked out of the police station in a nervous sweat. The other night he saw what he saw—no imagining it—and he headed home. He got home just in time to answer the phone, at which point his daughter informed him that she had met someone special.

Mike just smiled and thought, *I know, dear, good for you.*

When Mark got back to his place later that day he was in for a big surprise. The inside had been torn apart. Long black and brown animal hairs were all over the place, and the screen was punched out again. *That's enough,* Mark thought. He went into town and bought some cameras so that he could monitor the interior of his home. Later that night Mark fell asleep on the couch, and in the morning everything was even more torn up, and the screen was popped out again. Mark went to the cameras, slipped the DVD's out, and put them in his DVD player. What played made Mark's mouth drop open. He watched it twice to make sure, and then he called Mike.

"Mike, it's Mark. I think I need your help, and it's a bit weird."

"That's okay. Come on over as soon as possible."

When Mark got to Mike's place, he asked if he had a DVD player. Mike said yes and took the tape from Mark. They both watched the tape.

"Mike, I swear this isn't trick photograph or anything. It's just as I took it from the cameras I put in my living room."

"This is a lot to take in all at once, but I do understand."

Just then there was a knock at the door, and when Mike answered it Clara came in.

"Mark, I think you know my daughter, Clara."

"Mike's your dad, Clara?"

"Yes, Mark." She sat by Mark and kissed his cheek.

"Clara, I think it's time to clue Mark in on what has been happening in our area."

With that, Clara smiled, and Mark watched Clara slowly change into a beautiful white wolf who started licking his face and nuzzling his neck. Mark glanced back to Mike, who had changed into a huge gray wolf. Mark couldn't believe it! Mike changed back and told Mark, "Mark, we don't need a full moon to change, like in the stories and Hollywood movies. We change at will, and just like people there are good wolves and bad or evil wolves."

"So am I a wolf too, Mike?"

"Yes, you are, Mark, the one on the tape, and when you relax and will it to happen you will change."

"But why don't my clothes get all torn up when I change into a wolf?"

"That's more of stereotyping by Hollywood. You have to remember that matter is always conserved and never destroyed, so when you go back to human form your clothing stays the same."

Mark relaxed and let his mind float. Suddenly he could hear Mike and Clara talking to him, but they didn't move their mouths.

"Mark, you see we wolves use telepathy to communicate."

"I see." Mark looked down at his black-and-brown coat of fur and then at Clara as a wolf.

"I still think you're beautiful, Clara." He nuzzled her ears.

They all changed back and talked. Mike explained that he and Eddie from the gas station had been on a hunt with their parents, and both had been injured by a wolf on the trip. It was also true what the paramedics said about a wolf near the crash site when Mark crashed his car. It had been Mike.

"Mike, the paramedics said that if I hadn't been awake to tell them how badly I was hurt I might have died."

"I sensed good in you, Mark, so I tried to help, but I also infected you by licking your wounds to keep you awake."

"That's okay, Mike, you saved my life."

"There's an evil black wolf out there. Let's all change and go to the pond and let the evil wolf know we are here."

They all ran out of the cabin as wolves, met at the pond, and started the loudest and longest group of howls ever heard.

9

Far away the black wolf lifted its head and listened. *This can't be. There are three of them.* He took off toward the pond with rage in his heart.

"Why don't the three of us get together for breakfast tomorrow?" Mark asked.

"Mark, why don't you and Clara go? I have some errands to run early, okay?"

So Mark and Clara met the next morning for breakfast. As Mike watched the couple go off to the café, he was thinking that his daughter was in love with a good man. But the evil was still around that could destroy them all. If he could kill the black wolf on his own without endangering his daughter or Mark, their future peace would be ensured!

As the black wolf emerged from the forest, everything around the pond was still—no breeze, no insects, nothing—as though the stage had been set by fate! The black wolf smelled the other wolf coming, its wild musk growing stronger in the air. Suddenly on the far side of the pond a large gray wolf appeared and growled low and deep in his throat at the sight of the black wolf. The gray wolf sensed only one thing in the black wolf's mind, the urge to kill! At that instant the two wolves charged each other, their yellow eyes burning into each other, their growling growing louder as they leaped toward each other. Snarling, biting, and clawing ensued, with black and gray fur all over the place. Yelps of pain resounded as one or the other got hurt. The fight was short and ended in what might be called a draw. Both wolves retreated to the forest and disappeared.

As Clara and Mark were returning from breakfast, they noticed police cars in front of Mike's place and were met by Sheriff Mitchell, Mike's friend in the police department.

"Clara, I've got some bad news, hon," said the sheriff.

"Is dad okay?"

"No, he was attacked. We don't know by who."

"How is he, Sheriff?"

"He's at Salem Memorial and he's lost a lot of blood."

"Clara, let me take you to the hospital, okay?" Mark said.

Clara nodded and within an hour they were pulling into Salem Memorial hospital. The nurse in admitting directed them to the ICU, where they found Mike stitched and bandaged up. The doctor met with Mark and Clara outside the ICU.

"Miss, your father is very ill, and I don't just mean his injuries."

"What do you mean, Doctor?"

"Your father has a virus that is slowing his immune system. It doesn't react to any known treatment, and if we can't control it your father's health might be in question."

"Can we see my dad, Doctor?"

"Sure."

Mark and Clara went into room, which was quiet except for the noises coming from the hospital monitors. Clara held her dad's hand, and he opened his eyes and smiled.

"Hi, you two."

"Dad, what were you trying to do, taking on the black wolf all by yourself?"

"That's not important now, hon. What is, is that you and Mark need to go to the sacred well and bring me some of the water!"

"But, Mike, why is that so important, and what is this virus they say you have?"

"The virus is what makes us wolves, and the water I'm talking about is the only thing that can help people like us when we're injured by another wolf. Clara knows where one of the wells is. Its location has been passed down through generations of wolves who were entrusted with its location by the holy men of Indian tribes who lived in this area."

"Mike, how soon do you need the water?"

"Within three days, Mark, so you two need to get going."

With that Clara kissed her dad, and she and Mark headed home to pack for the trip that Clara told him would take a day and a half. The packing went fast, and soon they were at a deserted trail head. They walked until late afternoon, and Clara let Mark know they would be at the spring the next day. Clara led Mark off the trail the next day and up to a stone covered in vines.

"Come on in, Mark."

Clara disappeared through the vines. Mark walked through the vines, which closed tightly behind him, like they had a will of their own.

The sight that greeted him took his breath away. He stood next to Clara as she smiled.

"This is wonderful, Clara!"

"I'm glad you think so."

Mark stared at the luminescent cavern bathed in pale greenish-blue light from the well that was easily an acre across. Mark and Clara filled four gallon jugs and headed back to the trail head.

Once they got back they raced to Salem Memorial. The doctor had been trying to contact Clara about her dad's condition, so while the doctor talked to Clara, Mark went in Mike's room. Mark used a glass and poured some spring water into it from a well-hidden flask. For some reason it stayed icy cold.

"Mike, buddy, how would you like a really cold glass of water?"

"That would be great."

Mike sipped from the straw Mark had put in the glass of water. Mark held the glass until Mike finished it.

"Mark, I think I better have one more glass."

Mark filled the glass again, and once Mike finished it he motioned for Mark to come closer so that he could whisper to him.

"Mark, I can already feel it working inside me!"

Both Mark and Mike smiled big, and as Clara entered Mark explained what had just happened.

"Oh, Dad, I love you!" Tears rolled down Clara's cheeks.

"Listen, you two, I marked the black wolf for you, not as good as he got me but the person will have an injured left hand and a nasty cut along the left side of his face. You might check to see if anyone local has been out sick. It could be him."

Mark and Clara agreed to look and said their good-byes to Mike. On the way back through town Mark noticed the gas station was closed and a sign out front said GONE FISHING in big letters. Mark smiled to himself; he and Eddie had always liked fishing. Maybe he would stop by Eddie's place and see how he did, maybe get a fishing trip going with him.

The next day Mark stopped by the local bait store and talked a bit with Sam, the owner.

"Sam, I think I'll go visit Eddie and see how he did fishing."

"Well, I'd like to know where he's been fishing around here for three days!"

"You're kidding. He closed the station for three days?"

"You bet, and I haven't seen him buying any bait either!"

The hairs on the back of Mark's neck stiffened and stood on end. Could Eddie be the evil wolf? Just then Mark remembered Mike's story about him and Eddie getting hurt on a hunting trip as kids. Mark went to find Clara and told her what he found out.

"Clara, I'm going to run out to Eddie's today and see what I can see."

"Mark, please be careful!"

"I will, hon."

They kissed and Mark went home to pick up a couple of things he might need.

After Mark got directions to Eddie's place, he took off in his car on a back road so he wouldn't be observed as he approached Eddie's place.

Mark had brought the gun Mike gave him and a pair of binoculars. After getting to the spot he wanted, a hillside overlooking Eddie's place, he sat watching intently. More than an hour went by and Mark was ready to give up when the back door of Eddie's cabin opened and Eddie stepped out. Using the binoculars Mark could see Eddie's bandaged face and hand, but the worst was that as Eddie opened a shed door out back, Mark could see a deer hanging, like it had been shot but still had its pelt on. Eddie walked up to the carcass and ripped the hind quarter off with his bare hands. Then he took a bite of the raw flesh! Mark couldn't believe it. His childhood friend was the evil wolf! As Mark watched Eddie going back to his cabin, Eddie turned, his mouth bloody, and he stared right at Mark. Mark looked through the binoculars, and Eddie grinned a big bloody grin that caused Mark to break into a cold sweat, and then Eddie disappeared inside. Mark waited, to let his mind catch up with what he had just seen. Then he slowly made his way back to his car and went back to town as fast as he could manage.

Though older than Mark by a couple of years, Eddie had been Mark's friend and fishing buddy, but now all that would change. Eddie grinned when he got into the cabin and allowed himself to change into the black wolf just enough so that his powerful wolf jaws were available. Eddie needed his wolf jaws so he could crush the deer bone and get at the marrow inside. He drooled at the thought of the sweet marrow. As he ate, Eddie thought, *Yes, my good friend Mark, now you know who the black wolf is and I know who you are and just where to find you when the time is right.* Mark went straight to Clara's home and told her everything he had seen.

"Mark, do you think you and I together can take care of the evil wolf?"

Clara asked.

"I think we can if we are very careful. We should ask your dad for his advice too."

Clara and Mark arrived at the hospital to visit Mike. Mike's wounds were healing at a rapid rate, but he was still too weak to go with Mark and Clara to combat the evil wolf.

"Mark, back at my cabin there is a special talisman I keep in a lockbox. When you go up against the evil wolf I want you to wear it around your neck. It will help you."

"But what does it do?"

"It gives all transitional creatures, like us wolves, a boost of power, stamina, and protection against anything evil!"

Mike told Clara and Mark where to find the lockbox and gave them the key for it.

"Mark, when do you think the evil wolf will come looking for us?" Clara asked.

"I think it may be as soon as tonight. It was a mental impression I got from him when I was watching him through the binoculars. He wants us out of the way as soon as possible, so he'll be on the hunt for us."

"Well, let's go straight to my dad's cabin and get what we need and get ready, okay?"

The black wolf knew where Mark lived. After all, he had been there before. He would start his search there. Mark's home was dark and cold as the black wolf slinked through the shadows, making sure he wasn't there asleep, sniffing the air. Suddenly he caught a whiff of Mark, but it was mixed with a strong, wild, musky odor, a wolf odor! The black wolf started off slowly along the pond path. Could his friend also be a wolf?

This night was inky dark. The trees formed a solid canopy over the ground, and the only moonlight visible was over the pond. The trip to the pond took so long—stealth always did. The black wolf didn't come right out into the open but hung back at the forest edge, watching and smelling the air, his breath coming out in long plumes because of the cold. Clara put the talisman around Mark's neck before he changed. Then Mark relaxed and changed. Clara's eyes grew big as she watched Mark change into the same wolf he had been, but he was bigger by at least fifty pounds of pure muscle. Mark felt great as he watched Clara change, and they both went outside and walked quietly toward the pond.

They smelled the black wolf long before they got to the pond—a rancid foul odor, like rotting flesh. As they got to the pond, they watched the shore and finally saw a pair of yellow eyes. The pale yellow moon gave everything a slight yellow cast along with the ground fog. Both Clara and Mark stepped out into the open as wolves.

The black wolf slowly stepped out, snarling, plumes of breath boiling around his snout. Both Mark and Clara growled low in their throats, their own yellow eyes burning into the black wolf that was Eddie. Suddenly it became too much for Clara as she remembered what this wolf had done to her dad. She charged the black wolf by herself, leaping when she was six feet away as the larger black wolf rose up to meet her attack. The black wolf grabbed Clara hard by the nape of the neck and slammed her to the ground, making her bounce. Then he threw her body toward some rocks at the pond edge. Mark didn't know the condition of Clara; she didn't move. But he put one thought in his head and sent it straight at the black wolf: *You will die tonight!*

Mark and the black wolf circled each other slowly. Suddenly the black wolf reared up and charged Mark, coming down hard on his neck. But Mark tightened his neck muscles, forcing them to expand and forcing the black wolf's jaws to be forced open to the extreme. Mark leaped, threw his body back, and landed his weight on the black wolf hard, causing the black wolf to yelp. Mark smiled, knowing that he had withstood the black wolf's attack and made him yelp, but a wild grin appeared on the black wolf's face. Mark lunged at the black wolf, clawing and biting. Both wolves had bleeding wounds as they came apart. Then the black wolf, with its tongue hanging from exhaustion, charged Mark, and as he was just jumping over Mark, Mark leaped into the air, grabbed the black wolf's throat with all his might, and crushed it.

The black wolf fell into the pond, dead, and Mark walked over to where Clara lay. He bent down and noticed she was alive but hurt. He changed back to his human form and carried Clara back along the pond edge past the black wolf. It had changed back to human form, and it was

Eddie. Once they got to Mike's cabin, Clara and Mark drank some of the holy water to mend their wounds and then made a phone call to the police to report another animal attack out by the pond.

The police did their usual thing,checking prints and searching the area for witnesses.When Mike got out of the hospital he wanted to hear all about the fight. He was proud of both Mark and Clara.

"Mark, does this mean you will be leaving us for the big city again?"

Mark smiled as he looked into Clara's face and put his arm around her waist, hugging her gently.

"I've decided to make this my permanent home. I have a lot more to live for right here in Detroit."

With that, Clara kissed Mark deeply and Mike laughed out loud. Later in the day Mike's police friend was walking around the pond and looked up to see three of the biggest wolves he'd ever seen, grinning at him with their tongues hanging out. One was white, one black and brown, and the other one was gray. They didn't make any threatening moves but just grinned at him and then went into the forest.

NOVEMBER FIRST

I heard the beep of the alarm and rose to consciousness without opening my eyes. I lay in a strange bed and slowly opened my eyes. My vision cleared slowly. I was in a hospital room. The oxygen flowed through my nose tube with a quiet swish.

In the room with me was one of my friends, Dan. He was sleeping and had one leg in a cast. One of my arms and a leg were in a cast.

My name is Steve, and this is how November 2006 began for me . . .

My body felt heavy, and I was sore and sleepy. They must have given me something for pain. A nurse came in and checked Dan's vital signs and then came to me.

"We didn't expect you to be awake already, Steve, after all you've been through."

I tried to move and couldn't speak above a whisper. My voice cracked. "Are my mom and dad here?"

"Yes, I'll get them in a minute, okay?" the nurse said.

As the nurse carried on with her duties, I tried to remember exactly what happened. My mind seemed foggy. I got flashes of images, gross and horrible even to a twelve-year-old!

My mom and dad came in looking tired and a bit scared. As they stood beside my bed, they tried to talk to me. Their voices seemed to come down a long tunnel to me because of all the pain medication and the trauma.

"Steve, do you know how this happened to you and Dan?" they asked.

"Can't remember. Where did you find us?"

"We found both of you lying in our front yard with pillows under your injured arm, legs, and both your heads."

The nurse mentioned that I might recall more later after the trauma and medication wore off a bit.

After my parents left I tried to rest a bit, but a voice came to me across the room. It was my friend Dan. He was awake!

"Steve, do you remember what happened to the three of us?"

"No, Dan, and they haven't said a thing about Connie. The nurse said we might remember more after the drugs and shock wear off."

Both Dan and I lay back, quietly trying to make sense of the images our minds replayed back to us. Where was our friend Connie? I suddenly woke up screaming, nurses and orderlies tried to calm me down, and the only words anyone could make out were—"I remember!"

After they calmed me down, Dan started talking to me. "Steve, do you really remember it all?"

"I do. I wish I didn't, but I do, including the promise. Do you remember the promise?"

"I'm not sure. I remember making a promise but not about what."

"Dan, it was about Connie and why we can never tell anyone that she was with us!"

Dan stared at me hard, but I could see in his face he remembered, and then I saw my friend shiver.

It all started the week before Halloween. All the kids in our area looked forward to trick-or-treating, especially at Mrs. Duncon's home. She always made the most unusual and delicious treats, and since the three of us helped Mrs. Duncon during the summer with yard work, we got to sample a wide assortment of her treats throughout the year. One of my favorite treats was like a small cake, three inches long and covered with milk chocolate. When you bit into it, the cream it was filled with was ice cold and seemed to flow from the cake like slow-moving lava. I could suck on the end of the treat for five minutes before finishing the cream, and the cream was so cold, wisps of steam rose around my mouth as I ate it on the warm summer days. Whenever we ate them we all got brain freezes because the cream was so cold. Mrs. Duncon would just smile at us as we ate her goodies. Connie asked Mrs. Duncon if she would teach her how to make some of her secret treats

After a short pause she smiled and said, "Someday possibly, Connie."

I lived in Southeast Portland on Nehalem Street. My best friends lived close-by, and we palled around a lot. I lived across from Mrs. Duncon's place. Our street was special in that it had a cemetery at the end of it. Some sort of crap was always happening there—either gravestones being tipped over or homeless people sleeping on the cemetery grounds.

Mrs. Duncon was a nice person as far as we all knew, at least until a week before Halloween. Her yard looked dark even in the daytime, all year-round. From every angle the shadows seemed to obstruct the view and shift around, no matter your viewpoint—like those paintings of people where the eyes seem to follow you around the room. Her trees always looked dark against her home, no matter what kind they were or the color of their bark. Mrs. Duncon's yard was large and deep with a gate at the back, a large garden with a scarecrow, and a grapevine trellis attached to the home in back. The grapevines were so thick that they formed a canopy over her patio. I offered to trim them back, but she sternly warned me to *never* trim her grapevines. Her home looked small from the outside, but every time I visited I could have sworn it was bigger on the inside than on the outside.

On one of our visits, Mrs. Duncon told us she was having company. Her sister and brother were coming for a visit, so we were told we might not see much of her, since it had been a while since she had seen them. But she smiled and said, "I would like you to meet them once, okay?"

We all agreed, but I noticed Mrs. Duncon was very slyly smiling right at me. It made the hairs on my neck rise, and even though I was smiling, an inner voice was telling me to run away as fast as I could.

Three days before Halloween, Connie was so excited as she talked to me at school. "Steve, Mrs. Duncon invited us over to meet her brother and sister today. I already told Dan. He's coming. Can you?"

"Sure, let's meet in front of her house at five."

"We'll meet you there, Steve."

When we met, we were all pretty excited about meeting Mrs. Duncon's family. We rang the doorbell and Mrs. Duncon answered, wearing a long, dark purple shawl.

"Are you cold, Mrs. Duncon?" Connie asked. She smiled at her brother and sister, who smiled back.

"Yes, just a bit chilled."

Mrs. Duncon introduced us to her brother, Max, and sister, Eva. Max was pudgy and short but very pale. Gray hair saturated his sideburns, and his smile was friendly. Eva wore a black shawl. She was tall and slender and looked younger than Mrs. Duncon. We all sat and enjoyed snacks and a special bread her sister made, called probisha bread. The next thing I knew I was waking to the sound of laughter, and as I opened my eyes there sat Connie, Mrs. Duncon, and her brother and sister.

"Didn't you two get enough sleep last night?" Connie asked jokingly.

"I thought I did. Did both Dan and I fall asleep?"

"You sure did, right after eating the bread. I'm the only one of the three of us who stayed awake for our visit with Mrs. Duncon's family."

"That's okay, Connie. Maybe the boys will come back later when they're more rested, but it's late, and I think your parents might be worrying about you," said Mrs. Duncon.

I remember thinking it couldn't be that late. We had just gotten here. I looked at my watch, which said 8:00 p.m. We had been there three hours! I looked at Dan, and he looked just as surprised as me. So we said our good-byes. The next day when I got home from school Connie called me, and she was very scared.

"What's wrong, Connie?"

"I was cutting through the back gate at Mrs. Duncon's house today, and as I passed the scarecrow I swear its head turned in my direction. And as I watched it the eyes looked like they opened and blinked!"

"Are you sure you just weren't seeing things? After all, we were out late."

"No, I'm sure enough, Steve, that I never will cut through that yard again!"

At dinner that night my mom and dad were telling me to beware of strangers, since there had been some strange crimes occurring in our area lately.

"Like what kind of crimes?" I asked my parents.

I always was curious about things like that, and my mom and dad often shared the newspaper stories with me in colorful detail.

"Steve, lately a grave was dug up in the cemetery and the body stolen. One of the pillar stones in the church had been carved with a pentagram, and one of the homeless in the cemetery was found dead, murdered in a savage way."

"How was the homeless person murdered, Dad?"

My dad looked at my mom, who nodded to him.

"He had his throat ripped clean out."

I was dumbfounded when I heard all the news, not by the fact that we had crime in our area but by the strangeness of the activities.

The day before Halloween, my parents got a phone call and started asking me where Connie was or if I had seen her. I told them, "No, why?"

"That was Connie's parents. They filled a missing persons report because Connie never came home yesterday!"

That was the day Connie called me about the scarecrow. I called Dan. "Dan, Steve here, did you hear that Connie's missing?"

"Yeah, the police just talked to me and my parents. It's weird. Ever since Mrs. Duncon's family arrived, stuff's been happening."

"You don't suppose they had anything to do with Connie's disappearance, do you?"

"Well, it's the only change in our area recently that I know of."

"Dan, can you sneak out tonight? We need to find out what is going on with Mrs. Duncon and our friend!"

"Sure, Steve, about eight, okay?"

"See you then."

I met Dan a block down from Mrs. Duncon's house.

"Dan, Connie was scared of the scarecrow so much that she swore she wouldn't cut through Mrs. Duncon's yard ever again. I think we should check it out first."

As we walked over to the scarecrow, the moonlight filtered through the clouds overhead, giving everything a surreal appearance.

"Steve, this scarecrow is weird looking, and it smells funny."

"Yeah, I noticed the smell. Never smelled anything like that before."

"What's this on his shoulder?"

As Dan grabbed the stuff on the scarecrow's shoulder and looked at it, he shook his head.

"Steve, why would old lady Duncon put dirt on her scarecrow?"

"She wouldn't. It had to already be there when the scarecrow was put in."

Dan and I looked at each other and quietly backed away from the scarecrow, our minds churning a thousand thoughts a minute to try and explain this, and all the thoughts scared us to death.

"Steve, I want to leave."

"We can't, Dan, until we find out what happened to Connie!"

We saw light coming from some of the basement windows and peaked into the semilit room. One side had all sorts of bottles and flasks of different sizes. Some had fumes rising out of them, there were pots and pans everywhere, and way in the back was a long rectangle box that was open. Dan and I stepped to the back of the house and slipped inside the back door. We didn't hear the door shut, but if we had glanced up we would have seen two green vines holding the door so it wouldn't slam loudly. It was a trap, but we didn't know it. We heard voices as we moved quietly through the hallway. I knew them all. As we peeked into the living room we saw Mrs. Duncon, her sister, and Connie sitting, burning candles, and reading from a book that was so old the pages had yellowed.

Connie was dressed in a red shawl, Mrs. Duncon in purple, and Eva in black. Suddenly two pale hands grabbed Dan and me from behind. Like a vise, we couldn't break free as the fingers no doubt left bruises on our necks and we were ushered toward the living room.

"Max, did you get our two visitors?"

"Yes, I did, sis."

Max laughed an evil laugh, and as Dan and I looked at him we clearly saw the fangs in his mouth. Max was a vampire! Mrs. Duncon smiled and ordered Max to bring us in and seat us.

"So you two boys think you have a right to break into my home."

"Mrs. Duncon, we were just looking for our friend Connie," I said as Dan kept quiet.

"Well, Steve, you have found her. Maybe the reasons should come straight from Connie."

"Steve, when we ate the probisha bread that one evening it was a test to see if I was worthy to become a witch and join Mrs. Duncon's coven.

If you don't fall asleep after eating the bread you are one of the chosen. The scarecrow came to me in the night and gave me Mrs. Duncon's offer to join her coven. When I accepted, he brought me here."

"I believe you met my scarecrow, formerly a resident of the local cemetery."

Dan and I looked over to the body standing in the entrance to the hall as it groaned, the degree of decomposition very evident now! Both Dan and I felt like we were going to vomit from shock or the smell of the rotting scarecrow's corpse.

"Connie, don't you think you should get back to your cooking as we entertain your friends? Mrs. Duncon suggested.

Connie started out of the room, but before she made it all the way out an explosion came from the kitchen that knocked us all off our feet. A vile-smelling smoke came into the living room, and I heard Eva scream as she looked down at Max, his mouth agape, a piece of wood through his chest forced there by the explosion.

"Dan, come on. Let's get the hell out of here." I grabbed his arm. But as I moved and tried to grab Connie's arm, she jerked away from me and growled at me, her eyes showing malice.

Dan and I started to run for the hallway, but something in the smoke was distorting our vision and we were knocking into the hall walls. Behind us we heard Eva and Mrs. Duncon screaming at someone to stop us. Then we heard Max's voice booming and snarling. When we saw him enter the hallway as we hit the back door, the wood in his chest was gone and his fangs looked longer, saliva dripping from them.

Dan and I slammed the back door shut and tumbled into the cold night. The back door was barely shut when it exploded off its hinges as Max ran into it.

"Get those two busybodies," Max commanded.

We couldn't see who or what he was talking to. All Dan and I wanted to do was get out of there as fast as we could. All of a sudden we were grabbed by our ankles and lifted about six feet in the air. The whole family came to the patio, and Mrs. Duncon switched on a porch light. Now it was clear why Mrs. Duncon didn't want her vines trimmed; they were alive and at the coven's command.

Max told the vines to shake us up a bit. The vines did this with violent pleasure, knocking our bodies into the home and wooden pillars of the patio repeatedly. I think this was how we got so many broken bones, but I seem to remember a voice pleading not to kill us.

"Mrs. Duncon, please spare my friends. They know how to keep a secret, and I think with a gentle reminder on this day they will remember the promise for the rest of their lives," Connie said.

Then they all started laughing loudly with understanding. Connie and her new family placed us on the lawn and propped up our injured legs and arms. I like to think Connie did this because she still cared for Dan and me as her friends. And the promise was more like a posthypnotic suggestion to us in our state of pain: we must never reveal what happened to us or where Connie is, or Max would make a special visit to us—to dine on!

Dan and I had just finished talking, and visiting hours were almost done when I heard the swishing of long cloaks on the floor. The two people were wearing hooded cloaks, one purple and one red. I shuddered. I had seen those cloaks before. They came to my bed first and lowered their hoods. It was Connie and Mrs. Duncon, both smiling and looking radiant.

"Hi," Mrs. Duncon said. "Steve, I hope your injuries aren't too bad. We tried to make you comfortable after you were hurt."

"You really should thank Connie. She kept my sister and Max from killing you both, but her idea of reminding you of your promise was so special. We'll let Connie tell you herself."

"Steve, you and Dan are going to get a special gift on every Halloween from now on like this."

Connie took out a package for me and one for Dan, who was now wide awake and staring. I opened my box and inside were my favorite treats. The same went for Dan. We looked past the two witches.

"How long will this last, Connie?" I asked.

"Until you break your promise or your life ends, whichever comes first." And with that, both Connie and Mrs. Duncon vanished right in front of us.

Dan and I kept in touch over the years, usually by phone, and we talked about our special Halloween as we munched on our treats from our watchful witch friends.

A FRIEND IN DEED

The drive from the care center led Norman past the Mount Scott Park in Southeast Portland. Norman always liked this time of year, early spring, because of the sunshine and everything growing. The address on his trip sheet said that he was supposed to find 999 Woodstock. At times Norman had the toughest time locating addresses even though he had lived in Portland all his short twenty-three years, but as he made a right there was the home he was looking for: a modest ranch-style home with several chimneys.

Norman's job as a caregiver was special. He enjoyed helping people who were shut-ins for whatever reason, and he had advanced medical training that he earned as a paramedic.

Once he parked the car, Norman approached the front of the home. It seemed cooler than the surrounding sunlit area. He spoke into the intercom: "Hello, Norman from the caregivers center, Mr. Drake."

No one answered for a couple of minutes. As Norman was getting ready to try again, a voice full of age and dust came over the intercom: "Hello, young man, please do come in. The front door is open."

Shutting the door, Norman moved slowly into the home. It looked like an antique store from ages ago.

"Mr. Drake, where are you, sir?"

"I'm in the den along the hallway, straight ahead of you and to your left."

As Norman entered the den, he saw a man wrinkled by the ravages of time in his early eighties.

"My name is Norman, sir."

"And mine is Michael. Norman, how are you today?"

"Fine, sir."

"And, Norman, please call me Michael, okay?"

"Yes, okay."

"Did they tell you what I needed to have done?"

"Yes, Michael, they told me I'm to give you regular infusions of blood plasma twice a week until . . ."

Norman's voice trailed off. He was going to repeat the part he had been told about—*until Mr. Drake dies*—but the words dried up in his mouth. Michael seemed to find some pleasure in Norman's discomfort, and with a gleam in his eyes he boomed out loud, "I die!"

Norman was embarrassed by the old man's reaction.

"Norman, death is nothing to be afraid of. It's just a part of life and should be embraced, like your first kiss or your first serious love affair. Now let's get started. I have a feeling that you and I will be seeing a lot of each other, and I would enjoy having someone to talk to and share ideas with."

"Okay, Michael."

As Norman readied the IV and the plasma, Michael never flinched, but his eyes took in every action. That's when Norman noticed two things: Michael's eyeballs were yellow, like he had jaundice, and on the middle finger of Michael's left hand was a modestly ornate ruby ring with intricate carvings all over the band.

While the transfusion progressed, Norman wondered what country Mr. Drake was from, because he detected a slight accent.

"Michael, you have an unusual accent. Do you mind if I ask where you are from originally?"

"Originally I'm from a small Slavic country in Europe, which has changed its name many times throughout history. Norman, is this current job your career, or do you have higher ambitions?"

"Well, I hope to be a writer one day."

"What kind of stories do you think you will write?"

"Horror and mysteries."

"Do you have enough imagination for such an undertaking, Norman?"

The rest of the time Norman was at Mr. Drake's home, they talked in general about Portland. Then, with a slight smile on his face, Mr. Drake asked one more unusual question: "Norman, have you ever experienced a true horror mystery?"

"No, but I have a good imagination!"

With that, Michael burst out in laughter so loud and powerful Norman thought it would shake the windows. Michael kept watching him, the gleam in his eyes growing brighter, like an inner power source had been activated by Norman's presence.

"I can't wait till our next visit, Norman. Talking with you has made me feel years younger already!"

As Norman got into his car and started it, he wondered about his first day with old Mr. Drake and the questions he had asked him.

Two days later Norman got a phone call, canceling his appointment with Mr. Drake. It seemed that he had been injured and had a serious burn on his arm and that he should resume his standard visits on Monday. Norman felt lucky—an extra day off of paid leave. He found himself hoping that Michael's injury wasn't a result of a part of his home burning down. Norman was starting to like the old man he had just met.

When Norman visited Michael on Monday, a man in another car cut him off right in front of Michael's home. Norman flipped him off, but little did Norman know that behind him in one of the windows, Michael had been watching the altercation with a smile on his face as he let the curtain fall back into place.

By now Norman had permission from Michael to just enter when he arrived, and he did so now.

"Hi, Michael, Norman here. How are you feeling?"

"I'm just fine, Norman. My injury turned out to be less serious then they thought. Look, it's almost healed."

Norman couldn't believe it. Elderly people healed very slowly, and the care center had led him to believe that Michael was seriously injured. This was no more serious than a bad sunburn in just a couple of days.

"Michael, how do you manage to keep your home so clean? It must take a lot of time to keep it this spotless."

"I have a lady come in twice a week to clean. She is very good. Her name is Rosa. You might meet her. She's due in a few minutes."

Just then the front door opened and a female voice called out, "Mr. Drake, it's Rosa."

"Come in here, Rosa, and meet my friend Norman. He has been giving me my transfusions."

Rosa and I shook hands. She had a very infectious smile. Then she excused herself to start cleaning.

"It must take Rosa all day to clean your home, Michael."

"Yes, but she's a good worker and I pay her very well to be swift in her duties."

Norman got home that night and was feeling very poor. He thought he might have the flu. So he called in sick for the next three days, missing Mr. Drake's next two appointments. As Norman was in bed getting better, he received an unexpected phone call.

"Hello, Norman speaking."

"Hello, Norman, it's Michael. The center gave me your phone number because I was concerned about you and they didn't have any replacement to send me."

"I'm sorry about the problems, Michael. I came down with a nasty virus and have been bedridden for the last three days. Have you been able to get someone to get you your transfusions? Maybe Rosa could do it."

"Don't worry, I made other temporary arrangements until you get better. Do you think you will be able to come to my next appointment?"

"Oh yes, Michael, that will be for sure. You can count on it!"

"Good, I've missed talking with you."

A click on the phone let Norman know the conversation was over abruptly. Norman's next meeting with Michael wasn't for three days, and Norman knew Michael would need one transfusion between now and the next time Norman saw him.

One day before Norman was to see Michael again, Norman felt good enough to walk to the corner mini-mart and get the paper. It felt good getting out after being sick. When he got home he flipped the paper open to the front page, and there was a story about a murder that had police stumped. Not only was it vicious, but according to the article the victim was without any sign of how she was deposited in the park where she was found. There were no footprints or tire marks. Police said they were withholding the more grisly details of the murder of the housecleaning lady.

The next day Norman got a paper and confirmed his worst fears as he turned to the obituary page. A photo of Rosa was on the page, and the obituary noted she had no family in this area and that she was thirty years old. Reading this made the hair on Norman's neck stand up on end. How did he know it was Rosa when he first read about the murder, and why did he dread going to Mr. Drake's the next day? All Norman knew was that he would rather call Michael "Mr. Drake" and not a friendlier "Michael" for some weird reason.

When Norman arrived at Mr. Drake's home the next day, the home looked very dark, almost deserted. When Norman pressed the intercom button, Mr. Drake answered promptly, but there was something different about his voice. Norman entered and moved toward the den, where Mr. Drake usually sat on his recliner. The light was on in the den, but Mr. Drake was not there.

"Mr. Drake, are you here?"

From behind him Mr. Drake answered, "Of course I'm here, Norman, and I thought I asked you to call me Michael."

"Yes, you did, sir, but somehow it was making me feel a bit uncomfortable, especially since the loss of your housekeeper, Rosa."

"Hmmm . . . as you wish, Norman."

As Norman listened to Mr. Drake, he suddenly realized what was different about his voice. It wasn't full of dust, like when he had first met Mr. Drake. It was now smooth, strong, and even, as a man half his age. Mr. Drake smiled at Norman and sat in his recliner.

"Norman, is something wrong? You look bewildered."

"No, not at all. It's just that you seem much healthier today, and I thought you might be a bit depressed because of the loss of your housekeeper."

The smile never left Mr. Drake's face. "Well, it will be an inconvenience for a while until I leave."

"Since Rosa was your housekeeper for so long, I thought you would be mourning the loss of her."

"Norman, have you forgotten my attitude on life, that death—like life—should be experienced and embraced?"

"I thought that was just your philosophy."

"And as for Rosa, she was a wonderful person who I enjoyed, and it will be hard to replace her. I will have to wait till I'm back in my home country, where people like me are treated with awe."

"But why leave, Mr. Drake? Our country has its flaws, but we have the best medical care possible in the world."

Mr. Drake's eyes shined brightly as he listened to Norman. "In my country I will rejuvenate much quicker than if I stay here because of the special treatments a person like myself can receive from the people who understand me in my country."

Norman was getting a bit upset. No, he was getting pissed off! Mr. Drake had insulted his country and their doctors. "So just what makes you so damn special?"

"Norman, you should try and control your temper and respect your elders."

"You're just an old man who needs constant transfusions till he dies." Norman didn't mind saying it. He was so pissed, and all the while Mr. Drake just sat there, eyes gleaming and smiling slightly.

"Norman, you are half right. I am old, but do you really want to know the whole truth about me?"

"Sure, why not? It couldn't be that bad. After all, how bad does an eighty-year-old man get?"

Mr. Drake laughed out loud, and it shook the house. "Norman, you make me laugh so hard sometimes because of how uneducated you are in the history of the world."

"Well, why don't you educate me before you leave, Mr. Drake?"

"Okay, if you think you can handle it. I am old but haven't been a man for a long time. I am not eighty but eight hundred years old, and once every century I must return to my home country to rejuvenate myself for a new life."

"What do you mean you're not a man?"

Norman was ready to call the local mental ward to pick up Mr. Drake, until he spoke further. "Norman, I am a vampire! I know what you are thinking, and I'm not crazy. I was named after my great grandfather Dracula and changed it when I came to America."

"Did you kill Rosa, Mr. Drake?"

"Let's just say I found another method of getting my transfusions while you were sick."

"Were there others that you used as transfusions?"

"Yes, a few, and you're right that is the reason no footprints were discovered around the bodies in the parks. I have always loved parks! I realize that this is a lot to take in, but I hope to show you I am for real. Do you remember the day you flipped off the driver in front of my house when he cut you off?"

Norman just nodded his head.

"Well, giving someone the finger can be good or bad. In my country, it is a sign of good faith to a friend."

"What do you mean, Mr. Drake?"

Mr. Drake smiled and showed all his teeth, his fangs at full length. Norman watched as Mr. Drake took his finger with the ruby ring and pulled the whole finger off, ring and all, with a tearing sound. He wrapped the finger up in cloth. There was hardly any blood at all. He walked over to Norman and offered it to him. So scared he was shaking, Norman couldn't grasp the wrapped finger.

"Norman, you really should accept this. It's a special honor to you as my friend, and besides, you don't want to make me mad, do you?" Mr. Drake smiled, baring his fangs again. "There are some requirements with a gift like this. Never dispose of the finger. The ring you may wear. It will grant you success in whatever you do, and you will only age half a year for every year. Oh, and if I return and request the ring back, it must be returned to me upon request."

Norman nodded his agreement. At that point he just wanted to get out of that house and away from Mr. Drake. When Norman got home, he hid the wrapped-up finger and took a cold shower.

Twelve Years Later

Norman had to finish the chapter he was working on. It was the last one in his series of three books, all of which had been murder mysteries and done well enough so that he earned a good living. He tapped his finger on his computer, watching the ruby ring glisten in the light. For the first time in many years, Norman thought about Mr. Drake and wondered how he was doing. Suddenly, the phone rang. It seemed louder than normal, making Norman jump.

"Hello, Norman speaking."

"Well hello, Norman, how is your writing career coming along?"

Norman knew the voice—young, vibrant, strong.

"Hello, Mr. Drake, how are you?"

"Very good, Norman. It looks like you decided to wear my ring after all, from your writing successes."

"Yes, I did. It fits so well. Thank you."

"We need to get together and talk. Would tomorrow night be okay? Say, seven?"

Norman's mouth went dry, but he found his voice. "That would be fine, Mr. Drake."

Norman couldn't help but feel a bit trapped. What if Mr. Drake asked for his ring back? Norman had tried to remove it once, and it seemed it was welded right to his finger. The whole next day Norman couldn't believe how relaxed he was. When seven rolled around, he answered the doorbell quickly, with no fear.

There stood Mr. Drake, in his thirties, fit and strong, not wrinkled or gray like Norman remembered him when he had left.

"Please come in, Mr. Drake."

Mr. Drake came in and promptly sat in the biggest chair in the room. He smiled as he looked around and at Norman.

"What did you want to see me about, Mr. Drake?"

"Well, Norman, I came to ask for my ring back, per our agreement."

"I'm sorry, but it seems to be stuck to my finger."

"We can deal with that later. I noticed that all of your books have done well, but they are all murder mysteries. What about the horror you were looking to write?"

"I just couldn't get into it as much as the mysteries. I guess my imagination isn't as good as I thought."

"I'm sure that's not it. Maybe if you had a real-life experience, your ability to write horror would be better."

"Maybe, but how would I get that experience?"

Mr. Drake smiled wide, and Norman could see his razor-sharp fangs glistening.

"Norman, how badly do you want to write horror?"

"More than anything, Mr. Drake."

Mr. Drake explained to Norman that when a person is bitten by a vampire, he sees all the experiences of that vampire's life. If he is not killed by the bite, he remembers those experiences.

"What do you say, Norman? Would you like a lifetime of horror to write about as a gift from me to my friend for all your help and keeping my ring safe?"

Norman thought a moment and then laid his head on the arm of the chair that Mr. Drake was in. Norman was surprised the fangs were so sharp because he hardly felt them. When he woke in the morning, Mr. Drake had left a list of dos and don'ts for him as a new vampire. And there was a P.S. on the note. It read: *Thank you for my ring. Mr. Michael Drake.*

Norman looked at his finger, where the ring had been. He was missing the ring and his finger that it was on, but he was starting to remember the horrors of Mr. Drake's life. And as horror writers go, they were great inspirations!

BEWARE TALKING TO THE SOON-TO-BE DEAD

My name is Sam, and the incident I'm going to tell you about is one for which most people would accuse me of being crazy—unless you lived it, like me! I'm an average type of guy, casual, easygoing, and I work for a company that thinks greatly of its customers but not its employees. Most supervisors were very flexible when it came to the concerns of the people they supervised, but there was always that one exception that didn't follow the norm. This supervisor went off on her own tangent, making every encounter a futile effort, to the point that having dental surgery would have been much preferred.

This was a woman who some may have found attractive on the outside, but as soon as she spoke or acted, they realized just how ugly she was inside: Ms. Mildred Comfort. She had dark black, shoulder-length hair, walked with a strut, and made it a habit of talking down to the people she supervised, who she referred to in her derogatory tone as her "subordinates!" All of us in our department went out of our way to avoid dealing with her due to her narrow-minded ways.

It was close to Christmas, and the annual company party was coming close. It just so happened that I had asked for some leave time to spend with my family over the holiday, since we had nothing urgent pending. The night before the party, Ms. Comfort informed me that she wanted me to work on those days, collecting information from files that were part of her own duties. My jaw dropped, and I informed her that this was unreasonable, since I had put in for the time off two weeks prior. If she had told me then, I could have got the information before I left for the holidays. My face turned red with anger as I saw a slight smile creep across Ms. Comfort's face. I stormed out of the office before I said more and called my wife to tell her the bad news. I told my wife I would stay overtime if I had to, to collect the damn information in time to take my days off for the holidays to satisfy the cast-iron bitch!

I finished collecting the information for Ms. Comfort an hour after the company party started. The company parties were always fun, and everyone usually had a good time, so I stopped in to visit with friends and wish them a merry Christmas. The party was in full swing, and alcohol was flowing freely. After a couple of screwdrivers I was feeling good and lose. (I don't drink much since my college days.) I made a much-needed trip to the restroom, and I was greeted by the obvious sound of two people having enthusiastic sex. I recognized two of my coworkers having a very good time. She bent over the counter, with him behind her. They both smiled at me, and I smiled back and left to give them some privacy. That was the high point of my evening. From there it went rapidly downhill. I went to another restroom and then said my good-byes to the Christmas crowd. I made my way to the outer hall and was about to leave when a familiar voice called my name from behind.

"Sam, are you leaving already?"

It was Ms. Comfort, smiling at me.

"Did you finish the chore I gave you, or did you just ignore me again?"

"I finished your fucked-up chore, Mildred!"

I was drunk and didn't care what I said to her.

"Sam, I didn't give you permission to call me by my first name. At work I'm Ms. Comfort to those I supervise!"

"Oh shit, Mildred, it's after work. Relax your ass and loosen up a bit!"

"How dare you talk to me that way! I'll have you written up for the way you're talking to me!"

"*Me* written up? You have at least one couple in there that you know who are fucking they're brains out, just having fun!"

"Oh my gosh, Sam, I never—who are they?"

"I'm not going to rat on them, and maybe you should try it. It might just be the thing you need to relax and get rid of your nasty attitude toward the people you work around."

"No one talks to me that way!"

She stormed off, and I think I saw steam coming from her ears. I laughed to myself as I got in my car and left. I might have changed my behavior if I would have known what I had set in motion by my ranting at Ms. Comfort.

Early the next morning the phone was ringing off the hook, making my hangover more painful. (I told you I was a lightweight.) When I answered the phone, it was my friend Geoff at work.

"Hey, Sam, sorry to bother you on your holiday vacation, but I thought you might want to know what happened last night."

"What do you mean, Geoff?"

"Mildred Comfort had an accident while talking to a friend from human resources. They said she was very angry when the phone went dead. They found her sports car at the bottom of a thirty-foot cliff, smashed and burned. Mildred was dead!"

I fell silent. Did my comments to Mildred start things?

"Sam, a lot of people at the party heard that you and Mildred had an argument in the parking lot. Is that true?"

"Yeah, it is, and yes, I told her off and said that if she got laid once in a while she wouldn't be such an uptight nasty bitch."

"Well, you might get a visit from the cops. Just thought I'd warn you."

"What the hell! I wasn't driving her car. Besides, as fast as she drives, it was probably her fault, but thanks anyway, Geoff."

I poured myself a drink and told my wife what happened, even what I said to Mildred. My wife smirked a bit.

"At least you won't be coming home with heartburn anymore because of her."

"I guess so, hon."

Then my wife sat in my lap, wearing one of her short nightgowns, and smiled. "You know what you said to Mildred, about getting laid relaxing her and giving her a nicer attitude? Well, Sam, it's always worked for me."

With that, she smiled at me and kissed me, stood up, and took me to our bedroom, where we had a long, wonderful session of lovemaking.

The cops did show up at my home, and I answered all their questions. It turns out I was right. They said Mildred was doing fifty miles per hour on a thirty-five-mile-per-hour curve in the road, and it was slick with rain, causing her sports car to skid off the cliff. I finally relaxed and slept, but I was awakened by a most horrible guilt-ridden dream where I was sitting next to Mildred, coaxing her to drive faster and she did as I asked. Then I jumped from the car as it went into a skid. In my dream I could hear Mildred's scream and the crash as she hit the bottom of the cliff. I woke covered in sweat, my heart beating hard in my chest. It took me a few moments to settle myself down and relax again as I tried to convince myself that it wasn't my fault Mildred was dead. I rested and slept through the day but not restfully. My dreams were filled with all sorts of gross representations of Ms. Comfort as she burned alive, her bodily fluids boiling away as she screamed in agony. And in every dream she was always screaming the same word in anger—my name, long and drawn out, making me cringe as I woke from each dream.

My wife had finally gone to bed, giving up on trying to wake me. When I finally woke, the living room was mostly black except for the desk lamp that had been left on for me, casting a very low light. It took a while for my eyes to adjust. My mind replayed my last dream. All it amounted to was someone putting her arms around my shoulders, hugging me, but instead of a warm embrace it was ice cold. The only thing colder that I ever felt was the kiss on my cheek in the dream, so cold and dead the lips seemed to burn my cheek. That's the point at which I awoke and tried to adjust my eyes. I thought I saw something move in the black shadows.

"Is that you, hon?"

No answer. I decided to rest just one moment more, when I saw the whole top shelf of our modest bookcase empty itself of all its books and papers except the folder of information I had gathered for the late Ms. Comfort. I didn't think anything of this until much later.

When I returned to work I looked a bit unrested. I was still not sleeping well. Everyone went to Ms. Comfort's service, but not many were able to get up in front of everybody and honestly expound on her good qualities. I threw myself into my work and the dreams subsided, mostly. I finally told Jerry, one of my friends at work. I've known him since I was in high school, and after he heard the whole story he didn't laugh, tell me I was crazy, or rebuff me in any way. Jerry just took it all in like a longtime friend. Then he said, "Sam, this may sound a bit out in left field, but I had a similar problem concerning a late aunt, and I went to Colleen Rees."

"How is that in left field, Jerry? Is she a shrink?"

"No, she's a psychic!"

"You have to be kidding. You believe in that crap?"

"All I know is that she helped me with the tormented spirit of my aunt, and she made a believer of me. Here's her card if you want to talk with her."

I shook my head as Jerry left, doubting I would ever call the number. But one day later I was dialing from my office. The phone was picked up on the second ring, and a very professional voice answered. "Hello, Dr. Rees, can I help you?"

"Hello. A friend of mine suggested I call you after I relayed a story to him about someone who just died." There was a long pause.

"Sam, your friend Jerry was wise to direct you to me about this problem."

"How did you know who told me and who I was?"

Dr. Rees giggled and said, "Well, Jerry called me and relayed your story. It sounds very interesting, but I must warn you that when dealing with an angry spirit, things can get a bit nasty, very violent. Are you prepared for that?"

"Yes, if it means I'll be at peace again in my own self and daily life."

"Good. Meet me at the address on the card tomorrow at 11:00 a.m."

The phone clicked softly as she hung up, and I realized that I felt calm inside for the first time since Ms. Comfort's accident.

The address on the card belonged to a rustic two-story home right in the middle of town. A sign on the front of the home said DR. REES BY APPOINTMENT ONLY. I rang the doorbell and Dr. Rees opened the door with a smile.

"Hello, Sam, please come right in."

As I entered I was not prepared for what I saw: two walls filled, floor to ceiling, with books, diplomas from Stanford and Princeton, and curiosities throughout the room from around the world. Dr. Rees was unique, plump but very attractive, professional but with a sly, sexy smile, which I found to be pleasantly distracting at times.

"Sam, Jerry let me know some of the basics of your problem. Can you add anything to what he told me, anything that you may not have told him?"

"Dr. Rees, I didn't tell Jerry all the details of my dreams."

I told Dr. Rees every little detail of each dream, from the first to the last and including the night all the books came off my bookshelf. Dr. Rees was busy writing all the facts down. Then she stopped and was quiet for a long time.

"Sam, you have a couple of problems here. One, you think it's your fault for angering Ms. Comfort and causing her to drive recklessly. This is not your fault. Ms. Comfort had a history of speeding. You see, I've done some checking too."

I was dumbfounded, and my jaw dropped open.

"But, Sam, your biggest problem is with Ms. Comfort's ghost. She is blaming you and has become a poltergeist, directing her violence toward you and your family to pay for her death."

"I can't believe what you're saying, Dr. Rees. I've never come up against anything like this before. Can it be corrected in some way?"

"Yes. We have to perform a ceremony, and I know how this will sound, Sam, but if you want your life back we have to try this first."

I relented, and Dr. Rees gave me a list of items to bring. She advised that I should have Jerry help me since he had already gone through this.

As Jerry and I gathered some of Ms. Comfort's personal items from her desk area, we talked. "Jerry, how did you get access to Ms. Comfort's personal effects?"

"It's amazing what the guys in the mail room know and what they will give you access to for fifty bucks!"

"You're kidding, Jerry!"

"Nope. The mail room guys know everything that goes on in our company before we do, and they're all right people too."

We gathered all the items we needed, and I invited Jerry to come with me to Dr. Rees's office for the ceremony in two days. He agreed in a second. Considering what was to happen between the meeting and the time I got home that night, I wished I wouldn't have waited, for my sake or my family's.

After getting home, the evening went normal for a while. Everyone else had gone up to bed and I had fallen asleep in our living room.

Even though I didn't remember any dreams later, my wife told me she heard movement downstairs. She thought it was me being restless. It was close to midnight when I woke up and saw the shadow of someone moving across the room just out of the light. I couldn't understand how something could create a shadow without light. Suddenly a voice called my name slowly.

"SSSaammm!"

"What do you want? Who are you?"

No reply, just a strong breeze through the living room that smelled of wet decay and rot! I saw the figure again.

"If you don't leave I'm calling the cops!"

"Gooo right ahead and call them, Sam. Their laws don't apply to me."

"Laws apply to everybody."

"He he he, (light laughter) who said I'm a somebody?"

"Then what are you, and why are you here in my house?"

"Let me show you."

With that, the shadow figure came out of the dark, quickly stopping just three feet in front of me in all its horror: the torn, bleeding, and burned skin, cuts all along the body, and clothes ripped and hanging in tatters. But the most striking things were the hair and face. The hair stuck straight out from the skull, black with white streaks, and in those white streaks and the pale torn face light shades of green, A scream caught in my throat as I recognized the spirit visitor. It was Ms. Comfort, long since dead!

"Why are you here, Ms. Comfort?"

"Sam, you made me so furious with your shitty talk that I didn't pay attention to the road I'd been down a hundred times before. Now you and your family must pay for the hell you've put me through and into!"

"No, it was my fault. Don't blame my family!"

But there was no reply and a wind with the smell of rot on it assaulted my scense of smell. I found that there were no windows open to allow any wind in. The goose flesh on my arms was in panic mode. I woke my wife and told her the whole story. At first she thought I was just dreaming, but when we went to check on the children we found a bunch of wet waterweeds and a large piece of a blouse torn and singed by fire. I could see the horror run across my wife's face, and she made a call to her mother. Within an hour my family was out of the house and out of harm, I hoped.

The next day Jerry picked me up and we headed to Dr. Rees's.

When we arrived at Dr. Rees's office, I told both her and Jerry what had happened the night before. The doctor gathered Ms. Comfort's personal effects that we brought and put them into a tall narrow bowl. With the use of her own psychic ability, she started to make contact with the spirit of Ms. Comfort! At first it was like a slow whirlwind winding through the psychic's office, which gathered in intensity.

"No matter what happens, don't intervene with me and the spirit," Dr. Rees cautioned us.

Suddenly the items in the bowl started to glow, and the spirit of Ms. Comfort started to appear to our left, behind Dr. Rees.

The spirit hovered about a foot above the floor, and Dr. Rees seemed to be speaking in a strange language.

"Why have you human bags of shit bothered me!" the ghost yelled.

"We are here to send you into a relaxed plane of existence, Ms. Comfort," Dr. Rees said out loud.

"Not before I avenge the injustice that bastard, Sam, inflicted on me. He and his family must pay!"

The bowl with Ms. Comfort's things in it was glowing brightly, shooting a strong beam of light straight up out of the bowl. Suddenly Dr. Rees started a new incantation and was interrupted by the ghost of Ms. Comfort.

"Your words cannot decide if I stay or go, you psychic bitch!"

Suddenly Dr. Rees threw a handful of something on the floor, and it exploded in a small cloud of white smoke. The ghost screamed but was motionless. Dr. Rees leaned close to me and in a whisper, said, "Sam, the normal methods aren't working. If you want your family to be safe from this spirit, you must do exactly what I say when I tell you."

"What is it I need to do?"

"You must reach into the bowl when I tell you to, mold the substance into a ball, and throw it at the heart of the ghost. She has become so strong with hate for you that it is the only thing that will work. Now give me your hand."

As Dr. Rees took my hand, she seemed to have trouble breathing. She spoke some words and traced her fingers along my fingers. Suddenly the ghost was again moving at great speed, screaming with anger. Everything in the room that wasn't nailed down became airborne, making them dangerous projectiles. As we watched, Jerry was struck by an end table knocking him to the floor unconscious. The light from the bowl was white, and it looked like waves of heat were coming off of it, like you might see off of hot asphalt. Ms. Comfort's ghost started to move to me, knocking Dr. Rees out of the way. Dr. Rees screamed, "Do it now, Sam!"

With all the courage I could muster I plunged my hand into the white-hot mixture and screamed. The pain was intense.

"Sam, think of your family!" Dr. Rees yelled.

I smelled the burned flesh from my hand and did as Dr. Rees said. I made a ball of the burning white mass and threw it at the heart of the ghost when she was only a couple feet away. The ball hit the ghost dead in the chest and seemed to radiate bright light from its point of impact. The spirit screamed, and it shook the walls of the room. Then it was gone, and everything that was flying through the air dropped about us.

I went and tended to Jerry and Dr. Rees. My hand looked like a swollen raw piece of hamburger, wisps of smoke still coming off my fingers.

"Sam, let me take you to the hospital burn unit."

"And tell them what, Jerry? That I was playing with a flamethrower or killing off a ghost?"

"Sam, come to me. I have something special for your wounded hand," Dr. Rees said.

Dr. Rees had just a few bumps and bruises. She took a jar off a counter and spread the substance all over my hand. The stuff was the color of guacamole. Then she slipped a thin glove, seemingly made of silk, over my hand.

"Don't take this off for any reason for a week. Then you will be fine, Sam."

I agreed and took Jerry to the hospital. He seemed to be hurt worse than he thought, with a few broken bones. My family came home, and I told my wife what had happened. She was accepting all I told her with ease, considering what she had been told earlier. At the end of the week when I removed the glove, my hand was as good as new, except for a small C-shaped scar on the inside of my right index finger. When I asked Dr. Rees about it, she smiled and said, "All people who fight off spirits in this fashion are marked with the initial of the spirit they defeated."

I jokingly wondered how many initials Dr. Rees had. She just smiled at me and shook my hand, spreading her thumb and index finger apart. I looked and saw two rows of single initials along her index finger, the last one a new C.

Later that night my wife was telling me that some strange stuff was happening at her mom's home but all of a sudden it stopped.

"What kind of stuff, hon?"

"Oh, like the waterweeds we found in our place. Only we found them outside my mom's house. But as suddenly as it started, it stopped, and we couldn't find any weeds showing the ghost had visited us."

"What time did this happen?"

"About three in the afternoon. Why?"

"That was about the time that we were fighting off the ghost of Ms. Comfort."

EVOLUTION

Five hours ago a most unusual person was spotted by police, running along alleys and storefronts, smashing windows, and assaulting people at random. When the police trapped the person, the first thing they noticed was his rough-looking face and very heavy boned ridge over his eyes, topped off with long dirty hair. When the police approached him, he grabbed a piece of pipe and started threatening the police. That's when it went bad. Two officers were struck by the pipe, requiring hospital visits, and the unknown person ended up being fatally shot.

After the coroner viewed the body, he bagged and tagged him, keeping the victim from prying eyes and cameras. Once back to the morgue, Dr. James Doon made a call to his friend, Detective Mike Stoves.

"Hi, Mike, Jim at the morgue. Something just came up and I think you should come down here before I start an autopsy."

"It ... it's like nothing I've ever seen before, Jim?"

"Just get here as soon as you can, Mike. I'm keeping it out of the media's view until you have a chance to investigate."

"I'll be there in fifteen minutes."

Mike had never known Jim to overreact to a situation. He was always steadfast. So Mike started to worry about what he had found.

He walked into the morgue and went straight to the autopsy bay. Upon entering, Mike saw his longtime friend sitting on a stool next to a cloth-draped body dressed in his hospital greens.

"Hey, Jim, what's with all the mystery, bud?"

Jim motioned Mike closer and pulled the cloth down from the body.

Mike looked on in disbelief, his mouth agape.

"Jim, he looks just like the pictures we used to look at of prehistoric man, a Cro-Magnon!"

"That's why I called you. I've only seen bone structure like this on skeletons in the natural history museum, a caveman!"

"I don't see how this is possible. Could he be a mutation, Jim?"

"I don't know, but I intend to find out. I'm ordering a full analysis on this body, including x-rays."

"Well, let me know what you uncover. Call me on my cell anytime."

"Will do, Mike."

Mike went to leave the morgue but didn't even get out of the parking lot when a call came in for him. It was another series of violent assaults in a local bar. Mike arrived at the scene within ten minutes. The public had already been cleared away, and he showed his identification and entered the bar. It looked like a tornado had erupted in the center of the bar. Most of the tables and chairs had been smashed. Some were covered in blood, and a body was lying nearby, covered in a sheet.

Mike went to the officer in charge, who was making notes as fast as he could.

"Davis, what happened here?"

"From the patrons' statements, the guy under the sheet came in wearing just shorts. When the manager told him he would have to leave unless he could dress more appropriately, the guy on the floor clubbed the manager over the head with a chair and then proceeded to destroy the rest of the place using parts of the bar to smash the other patrons. We have eight headed to the hospital with injuries."

Mike knelt next to the sheet-covered body and lifted the piece covering the head. He shook his head and ordered Officer Davis to seal the scene to the media. As he walked away he called his friend at the morgue.

"Jim, we have another one."

"You mean a crazy caveman?"

"That's right, and this time people were hurt as a result."

As Mike ended the call, he could only wonder what the hell was going on in this city in which he grew up.

When Mike arrived at work at the Portland Police Center, he was greeted by no less than twelve messages from the morgue. Mike wondered why his friend hadn't called his cell phone. Then he remembered that he had turned off his cell a couple of nights ago when he had been on a date with his girlfriend, Jenny. He smiled to himself as he turned his cell back on. When he was with Jenny, she was the only distraction he wanted.

Mike decided to go to the morgue and see what all the fuss was to warrant all these messages. As Mike walked into Jim's office, he found him napping quietly. He sat down across from his friend, smiling. Slowly Jim awoke and saw Mike.

"Mike, it doesn't do any good to have your cell number when your cells turned off."

"Sorry, Jim, so what's the big news?"

"In both of the bodies from last night, an x-ray revealed a small computer chip at the base of the brain, more sophisticated than I have ever seen."

"You're kidding, aren't you, Jim? This sounds like science fiction."

"Do the dark circles under my eyes look like I'm kidding, Mike?"

"No, how could something like this happen?"

"My guess is someone is doing experiments on humans, an interest either government or private company with a lot of money to burn."

"Can you remove the two chips, photograph them, and let me show them to our people in cyber?"

"It's already done."

Jim handed Mike a small bag with the chips, and Mike called the computer experts at the police station. When Mike showed his friends in the computer department the chips, they couldn't believe it. Bill Donaldson told him that the computer chips had been traced through serial numbers back to a lot that was purchased by the military and that the chips were used for research when people applied for grants through the military.

"But, Mike, that's not the strange thing about these chips. What's strange is that the chips were general-purpose chips, like for any everyday

 46

computer. But then they underwent some extreme modifications that we can't even begin to guess the functions of."

Bill showed the chips to Mike under magnification and pointed out several relays and nodes that were added when compared with a regular chip. Mike contacted the military, and with the batch number they located who the chips were issued to for research, a Dr. Mon at the center for behavioral studies. The next morning Mike and Jim went to the center and met with Dr. Mon.

"Dr. Mon, I'm detective Stoves, and this is our coroner, Dr. Doon. We have some questions about some computer chips you purchased last month."

"It seems that we found two of the chips that you had purchased in two rather unique individuals who went into rampages in our town. Can you tell us about what kind of research you're doing?"

"Well, Mr. Stoves, those particular chips were being used in some classified research. I'm afraid I can't tell you more due to national security."

"But, Dr. Mon, the presence of the chips wasn't the only unusual aspect of the individuals. Their appearance was strikingly like prehistoric man."

"Dr. Doon, this all sounds like science fiction. Maybe you two have been working too hard."

"Dr. Mon, we both saw the individuals and the havoc they caused and the people they injured. This is no joke. We want to know what your research involves."

Dr. Mon's face grew stern and grim. "If you two want to know what our research is about, you had better get a warrant. Otherwise get the hell out of my office with this garbage you're spouting."

"Okay for now, Dr. Mon, but we will be back. Don't leave the city."

Dr. Mon sat at his desk and called a private number. "Yes, Dr. Mon here. The police and coroner were just here, asking me about our government program 321 . . . No, we don't need to shut down. Just go forward with our plans, as usual."

After Dr. Mon got off the phone, he smiled to himself. *Who do those assholes think they are threatening with a warrant?* Then he made a call to his friend in the CIA and explained the problem.

Because Mike and Jim furnished photos with their application to the judge for the search warrant, it was granted just as some government officials came into the court to stop it. The government officials tried to have the judge reverse his ruling, but he refused.

"We can't have dangerous research being done in our city that could cause its population harm."

Mike and Jim left for the behavioral center with the warrant and a supply of officers.

As Mike and Jim arrived at the center, they were greeted by a guard at a closed gate. The guard didn't offer to open the gate but wanted to know their business. Instead of explaining to the guard, Mike just showed him the search warrant and the guard slowly went to the control shack, smiling and keying the gate open. Then he pressed a red button under the counter that sent an alert signal directly to Dr. Mon's office. Dr. Mon smiled and took an express elevator to the bottom floor, three levels below the main facility. As the doctor stepped out of the elevator, he was greeted by a directory of labs, storage areas, and research and development areas. Dr. Mon headed to the computer hub storage area.

As Mike, Jim, and six police cars pulled up in front of the center, Mike gave them all instructions to search for any research documents or computer files. After an hour, the group of officers, including Mike, had only found some interesting items referring to a project called "Evolution," but nothing else. Then they entered Dr. Mon's office by force. It had been sealed electronically. When they entered, his computer files were gone and so was he. Mike took as many people into the express elevator as he could and went to the bottom floor. Upon arriving, they read the directory and spread out to each room. When they reached the first of the rooms, the people there were surprised. Dr. Mon had run and left them there to whatever fate the police would dictate.

"Jim, have you ever seen anything like this before?"

"No, and it's important that we try to recover any project files, notes, or disks to get a handle on what this nut was really doing."

"Attention, all of you, Dr. Mon is a person of interest and we are searching for him in relation to possible criminal charges about his work here. If any of you can help us sort this mess out, your cooperation will be noted later.", as Mike addressed the employees.

At first no one came forward. Then a young scientist stepped up. Her name was Mary Jacobs.

"Detective, would it be helpful to have copies of the research project computer disks?"

"Of course it would. Come with me."

"Miss Jacobs, why did you make copies of the project disks?"

"My brother was a scout and I like to be prepared. Besides, some of the good doctors' explanations for our research didn't sound very plausible, so I decided to cover my ass and make copies of everything we did secretly."

Mike and Jim were smiling from ear to ear as Mary took them to where she had the copies. She had made copies on data sticks, which were small enough to hide. There were two dozen sticks with hundreds of files, and they were labeled. Both Mike and Jim snagged the one labeled PROJECT OUTLINE and went to a computer port they could use. As they read the file, they couldn't believe what Dr. Mon was doing. According to the disk he was turning healthy people into prehistoric individuals, because they were stronger and could take more physical punishment than a normal person. Then they were given various levels of training through the computer chip at the base of their brain. This was activated at the behavioral center's whim, and the programming would run.

"Mike, he was creating supersoldiers by reversing the evolutionary lines and using his own special mix of drugs, and he was experimenting with causing a human to progress ahead along the evolutionary lines. See, they already had some successes with increased brain function, paranormal abilities, and healing ability."

"Jim, do you think the military was involved?"

"I would say that's confirmed by all the generals and CIA personnel they seem to have to report to."

"How do you know the CIA is involved?"

"I recognize one of the names. That's who he works for now. I thought he was my friend."

As everyone left the center with all the documentation, the guard at the gate shack received a phone call. "Have they left yet?"

"Yes, Dr. Mon, but I think you should know that they took a lot of files, and I overheard someone saying that one of the researchers offered the cops copies of the project."

"Holy fuck, how did that happen?"

"Someone was copying our files as a bargaining chip. What do you want me to do, Doctor?"

"Find out who leaked the files, and report to me. I'll be at the second site."

"Okay, Doctor."

Mike was riding with Jim and thinking out loud. "How did the good doctor know we were there? The coffee in his cup was still warm, so he had just left."

"Who was the first person who saw us arrive?"

"Shit, the guard at the entrance must have alerted him."

Mike radioed to the patrol cars still at the scene to pick up the guard from the entrance and bring him in for questioning.

Mike was questioning the guard when he got an emergency call from Jim.

"Mike, we have another evolution man. Only this time there were two victims of his attack."

"Who, Jim?"

"It was Mary Jacobs right out in front of the station and Jenny."

When Mike heard Jenny's name, he froze. "Is Jenny okay?"

"A couple of broken bones. She needs to stay in the hospital a couple of days."

"What about Mary Jacobs?"

"Mike, she's dead. She was attacked along with Jenny outside our station. Mary's body was thrown into a concrete wall, snapping her neck right after we got her signed statement. I've got Mary and this other guy on separate slabs in the morgue. Why don't you go see Jenny."

Mike was out the door of the morgue and at the hospital before he knew it. Jenny's doctor confirmed what Jim had told him, and Mike took a seat. Jenny didn't wake for an hour, and Mike's face was the first one she saw. He kissed her gently around her bruises.

"How are you doing, hon?"

In a low voice, she said, "About as good as I look. What about the other girl?"

"She didn't make it, Jenny. She was one of our witnesses on a case I'm working on."

Jenny fell back asleep quickly, and Mike went back to the station. He called in and told them to have the guard ready for more questioning as soon as he got there.

Mike entered the room with the guard, who was nervous, having been brought in for questioning twice in one night.

"Well, you know your Dr. Mon unleashed one of his freaks on someone I care very much about tonight."

"What's that got to do with me?"

"Well, the lady who made the tapes secretly was the other victim. She's dead. What do you think Dr. Mon is going to do to you when we let the media know we have you and you're talking?"

"You can't do that. He's crazy. He'll do anything to protect the project. He would have me killed somehow!"

Mike slammed his fist down hard on the table in front of the guard. "Then you better start talking or I'm going to have you put in general population in prison!"

The guard was quiet for all of five seconds. "I need protection from this nutcase and reduced charges. Then I'll tell you everything."

After talking with the guard, Mike got the necessary warrants and a SWAT team to hit Dr. Mon's second site. It was twenty minutes out of town, and this time they brought a helicopter full of cops to secure the area. When they arrived they sealed off the compound and herded as many people together as possible. They found a locked lab underground, and they used explosives to open it and entered. Shapes moved at the back of the room, and three massive fire bombs went off, causing everyone to dive for cover. By the time the fires were under control, only half the lab was left, but it was enough. Burned containers with failed experiments of previous evolution men were grotesquely displayed, and they found more records. As Mike was reading the first of the records, he heard movement behind him. He dove and just missed getting shot in the back. Mike put two shots into the shape firing, and he went down. Mike went to the person, and it was Dr. Mon. He was dying and he smiled, motioning Mike closer.

"Detective, there is still one more center out there, making my monsters for the government."

"The hell you say. Where is it, Dr. Mon? Where?"

With that, Dr. Mon died smiling, not saying a thing as Mike shook him.

A month later, Mike was promoted because of his work on solving the Dr. Mon case. Jenny was better, and they were going to have dinner. Mike was planning to propose to Jenny over dinner. As Mike went out of the station, he glanced up at the full moon. The air smelled good. Then on the top of the building across the street a shadow appeared and looked down at him and waved. It turned to a profile and Mike's jaw fell open. He had seen that prehistoric head shape before and long stringy hair. It was another evolution man. It was starting again!

FATHER S DAY

My name is Stan, and in the last year my outlook on life in general has become dismal. It all started last year when my mom died after fighting cancer for two years. My favorite dog, Roco, died just two weeks before my mom died. It's hard to lose members of your family so close together. It leaves a lot of emptiness in your life with nothing to fill it in. My dad had died when I was just thirty. He was a very unique person. My parents were both unique in how they raised our family. They believed in being open-minded to the possibility of things that some people wouldn't allow their kids to believe in.

My dad, for instance, believed in the aspect of spirits, psychics, ESP, and dreams through which loved ones could communicate. My youngest sister was even named because of a dream my dad had in which his dead brother came to him, told him her gender, and said her name was Frances. So when my youngest sister Frances was born, we all were amazed, except my dad. He just smiled and told us he already knew from the dream.

One summer evening I decided to take a long walk in the local high school field near where my family and I lived. It was completely dark when I started back home, hoping the fresh air would clear my head and cheer me up a bit. As I walked along the cyclone fence at the back edge of the field, I was surprised when I saw a small round, light glow up ahead appear and go out. Then it appeared again and went out. Then

I smelled the cigarette smoke. Someone was sitting outside his yard having a smoke. Funny, I hadn't noticed them before. I moved away from the fence so I wouldn't run into the sitting person, who spoke to me in a gravelly tone of voice. "Hello there, young man."

I smiled at the words he used, because I'm fifty-three years old. Normally people I meet don't call me young anymore.

"Hello," I replied.

"So are you just getting some fresh air, or is something on your mind tonight?"

"Just a bit of both."

The fellow smoked slowly, and I had a sense of déjà vu making the hair on my neck stand on end.

"My name is Ed. What is yours?"

"Mine is Stan. Glad to meet you."

I shook Ed's hand. It was like holding a hand full of dry leaves, but with a friendly grip.

"Stan, I'm just visiting in the area and I was wondering if you're the type of person who likes to sit and visit."

"Well, some people say I have the gift of gab."

Laughing, Ed asked, "How would you like to visit with me over the next three days? We could just shoot the breeze."

"I wouldn't mind that at all."

Privately I thought this might take my mind off of things, distracting me in a healthy way. Ed and I agreed to meet the next night at the same time and parted company.

On the next evening, I moved into the field of the high school quietly, hoping to see where Ed came from. I looked all around and didn't see any sign of him.

Then as I looked to my left, an outline of a man sitting showed in the darkness.

"Ed, is that you?" I asked.

Then I saw the red ember of the cigarette glow brightly. It gave me goose flesh because I could have sworn I already looked in that direction a few seconds ago.

"Ha ha ha. Yes, Stan, it's me. Come closer, please."

I moved closer and sat on the dry grass in front of him. The grass was crisp and rustled as I sat, dry from the summer heat.

"Well, Stan, what should we talk about tonight?"

"Anything. I have a lot of interests."

As we talked, the smoke from Ed's cigarette seemed very familiar.

"Ed, what kind of cigarettes do you smoke?"

"Why?"

"Well, they smell just like the kind my dad used to smoke. It kind of brings back memories."

Ed showed me the package. They were the same as my dad used to smoke.

"Stan, what kind of work are you involved with?"

"I work in the biological sciences in a lab. What do you do?"

"I'm long since retired, you might say, but I used to be involved in the grocery business."

"To work in the sciences, you must have a very open mind to new situations."

"Sometimes, Ed, but sometimes I just don't know why things happen when they do. Whether it's fate or luck, it messes with my mind sometimes."

"What do you mean?"

"Well, like when my mom died a year ago, I know they did all they could for her, but two weeks before she died my favorite dog, Roco, had to be put down because he had leukemia."

"Maybe Roco was to act as kind of a guide for your mom after she passed away."

"I never even considered that. All I could think of was how two important spirits in my life had been taken from me in one quick swoop."

"Stan, do you think the idea of your dog guiding your mom is ridiculous?"

"Not at all. Actually, the idea that they are together makes me feel better."

"Good. Feeling good after losing loved ones is important to the living and to the dead."

After Ed's statement I was quiet for a moment. Then I asked, "What do you mean?"

"It's just that I believe those that die before us can still check in on us every now and again to make sure we are doing okay. I think it might give them some satisfaction to see their loved ones moving forward."

"Well, if the people I have known who have passed away look in on me, I hope they aren't too disappointed."

"Stan, I'm sure that they are more than proud of you . . . if they're looking in."

I couldn't figure out why Ed paused when he did, and for what seemed like a half hour, when I'm sure it was just a few seconds.

"Stan, I have to be getting inside. I'll see you tomorrow, okay?"

"Sure, Ed, I really enjoyed talking with you tonight."

But Ed and his chair were already gone. How could he do that? I just turned to leave for a second and suddenly he was gone. Then I smelled it, a smoldering cigarette butt at my feet. I picked it up, but it was crushed out, as if between two fingers. How could he do that without me seeing him? As I walked back to our apartment, I wondered if all this was a stress-induced dream. It felt very weird, but all I knew was that every time I talked with Ed I left feeling better than when I came.

When the next night came, I noticed that the moon was almost full. I thought at last I would be able to see the face of the stranger with whom I had been talking. When I heard Ed call my name, I turned, thinking I would look right in his face. I was very curious. But as soon as I looked toward Ed's face, the sky clouded over, blocking out the glow from the moon. Ed's face was again in shadow!

"Stan, are you trying to see what this old man looks like?"

"Well, yes, I was kind of curious. It comes from working in the sciences."

"You were always curious about new things, especially science."

"What do you mean, Ed?"

"Sorry, I meant to say you are curious about all new things, especially since you're in the science field."

I knew what I heard. Something funny was going on here. Ed changed the topic quickly.

"Stan, tell me about your family. Are you married?"

"I have been married twice. My first wife passed away unexpectedly, but I was very lucky to find another wife to love me just as much, if not more."

Ed was silent for a few minutes, just puffing on his cigarette slowly.

"It's good that you found another lady to share your life with. In the grander scheme of things, happiness and love are what help us live our lives."

 56

I was looking up at the single mass of clouds blocking the light of the moon. It didn't seem to be moving with the few other clouds around, even though there was a slight breeze.

"Stan, do you look up at the night sky often in the middle of a conversation?"

"Sorry, I was distracted by the clouds blocking out the moonlight. They don't seem to be moving."

Ed just laughed lightly, like there was a joke that only he was aware of. "Stan, you will be able to visit me tomorrow, won't you? After all, it's Father's Day."

"Sure, I'll be there."

And no sooner had I said I would be there than Ed's shadow mixed into the darkness surrounding us, and the clouds unblocked the light of the moon. There had been no sound of movement, no rustle of a chair folding up. He was just gone! I sat for a long time, trying to figure things out in my head. I didn't feel at ease. As usual I felt creepy, with goose bumps along my arms and my neck hairs standing on end. I was beginning to doubt my own state of mind. Maybe the stress of the last year had been too much and I had finally taken a little trip into left field for a little time-out. When I reached my home I was covered in a cold sweat, the type that makes your clothes cling to you after a nightmare.

It was Father's Day, and as evening drew near I started shaking a bit, remembering the events of last night. I went out the door and it was pitch black. The moon was full but blocked by a heavy layer of overcast. I wouldn't be getting a glimpse of my mysterious friend tonight. As I entered the field, I saw the glow from Ed's cigarette right away.

"Hi, Ed, happy Fathers Day!"

"The same to you, Stan. Are you having a good Father's Day?"

"Yes, I'm having a very good day. My kids came to visit and they gave me gift cards to buy gear for my favorite sport, fishing. How about your family? Did they visit you?"

"Actually, you've been my only visitor today. It's kind of hard for the rest of my family to visit me due to the distance."

"Well, I don't mind visiting with you, especially today."

"Thanks, Corky, I really appreciate that."

"Ed, what the hell is going on here? Nobody has called me Corky since my dad, and only members of our family knew that he used that nickname for me!"

"I'm afraid I've been deceiving you a bit for your own good. You see, I wasn't sure how you would react in a situation like this."

"Like what?"

"I know you have wanted to see my face, but I made it impossible for that to happen on our visits, which I have enjoyed very much. Do you still want to see my face? If you do, I will allow it."

"Yes, Ed, and since I'm not a cat my curiosity won't kill me."

Ed laughed a little at that. Then the clouds spread open so the moonlight cascaded all over Ed, showing his whole body in detail.

My mouth fell open and Ed's face broke into a huge grin.

"Dad! How can this be? You were dead a long time ago!"

"Stan, I just wanted to visit you and see how you're doing after having such a rough year."

Tears started rolling down my cheeks, glistening in the moonlight.

"Stan, I have missed you and being around you as you grew up and had your career. All of us have."

I got it now. My dad's middle name was Edward.

"What do you mean 'all of us have,' Dad?"

"All of us who were close to you and have passed away have been watching over you, and although not everyone could come to visit you like me, two could."

With that, my dad threw a ball into the dark and I heard paws running toward me. Suddenly out of the dark, a dog with a gray-and-black mottled coat, a white blaze on his chest, and white paws started jumping right in front of me, happy to see me. It was Roco! I hugged him close as he licked my ears, and I felt his wet nose nuzzle my neck. Then there was movement from the corner of my eye, and someone else came into the moonlight. It was my mom! She walked slowly to me, hugged me, and whispered, "It's all right, Stan. I'm without any pain, and I have your dad and your first wife to keep me happy here. By the way, your first wife asked me to give you this."

My mom kissed my cheek and slipped a small heart encrusted with diamonds into my hand. We could never find it after she passed away.

I hugged my mom tightly, and although she felt cold, it made me warm inside.

"Stan, we have to be going soon, but I wonder if it would be okay to visit you from time to time?"

"Of course," I whispered.

"All of us are looking out for you, and just so you know we are all very, very proud of you and the person you've become."

With that, the three of them, standing in moonlight, started to fade into wisps of fog and smiled and waved at me. There was no doubt in my mind that I had been visited by three ghosts, but to punctuate their departure a cigarette butt was flicked out of the darkness where they had been standing. I picked it up and looked at the brand and smelled. Yes, it was my dad's brand. I smiled.

REVENGE

Chicago was a rip-roaring town in 1929. It had every aspect of life, including gangs. The people of the Windy City had grown used to gangsters being killed one or two at a time. But on one day in February, seven gangsters were lured to a Lincoln Park address where they were gunned down by machine guns. The public was outraged by the sheer boldness of the act in which two hundred shell casings were found. The police determined about half of those bullets went through bodies before they struck the wall behind them. No one was ever convicted of the killings, but the people of Chicago had their suspicions.

Because of the nature of the killings, rumors grew about the bricks in the wall, about how they brought bad luck and misfortune to anyone who passed them. Everyone in Chicago had heard about the bricks and the curse that went along with them. Children grew up knowing about the bricks.

Present Day

Mike, Ben, and Sarah had all grown up together and gone to the same schools, and now Ben and Sarah had been married for five years.

They all remained friends and enjoyed doing things together. Ben was reading the paper before going to work when he spotted an article about the massacred bricks that were going to be used as part of a wall in a nightclub, Ben took the paper with him as he headed to work.

One day he took off early from work and headed home. He had a pounding headache. As he pulled near his home he noticed Mike's car parked down the street. What was Mike doing there in the middle of the afternoon?

Ben heard noises coming from inside and went around back to see what was going on. As he peeked around the corner of the sliding glass door, Ben's mouth dropped wide open with shock. He had to bite his tongue, he was so shocked! There was his wife, Sarah, and his best friend not just making love, but fucking in the nastiest ways. Sarah was doing things with his best friend that he had asked Sarah to do to him, but she had declined. Ben pulled back and walked to his car, the rage building with every second. *I am going to get back at those two, God damn it!* Ben headed to a bar to kill a few hours and think of a way to get back at his wife and best friend, Mike. Maybe he would have just one drink and mull it over. Ben got up to use the restroom and passed a brick wall in the bar. It was the wall he had read about in the paper. He hadn't even realized what bar he was in.

Ben started to figure out a way to get back at Mike. Ben went back home and was greeted by Sarah. "Hi, Ben, how was your day?"

"Just fine, long and hard. How about your day?"

"Oh, it was just a regular day. Got to lie around. It was nice."

Ben thought to himself, *Yeah, you bitch, lying down while my best friend fucks your brains out!* Ben just smiled and went to the shower. In the shower he made the water as hot as he could stand it. The warm pain helped ease his rage. After the shower, he and Sarah ate dinner. Sarah made an excuse of a headache and went to bed early. Ben sat up and tried to figure out if the crazy idea he had would work. To accomplish his plan he would have to hire someone with special skills. Ben smiled a very satisfying smile the more he thought about his plan, *Revenge!*

The next day Ben contacted a friend from the neighborhood in which he grew up. His friend was known to police by several aliases. Ben told him what he wanted, and his friend just laughed and agreed to a price and delivery date. In two days, Ben had what he wanted from his criminal friend, and they parted company. Ben looked at the items. Coincidentally, the items had the year they were made imprinted on them. Ben thought it was a nice touch.

One afternoon Ben left early and drove to within a block of his home. He was fairly sure that Mike and Sarah would be preoccupied, so he could finish his plan. Ben saw Mike's car in his driveway and checked the car door. It was unlocked. Ben slipped the items under the driver's side seat. He thought to himself, *If this works, in a couple of months Mike's going to be looking at life a bit differently, and if it doesn't work, Mike will just have a mystery on his hands.*

After about a month, Ben noticed Mike's skin was becoming paler, and Sarah seemed to be more on edge lately.

"Sarah, have you been all right? You seem kind of down."

"I'm fine. I'm worried about Mike. He stopped by and he looks like he lost weight and he doesn't look good."

Inside, Ben was smiling to himself. *My god, is this really happening?* Ben felt like celebrating and made some excuse to go out. He went over to the home of his personal secretary, Judy. She had made it more than a little obvious that she was attracted to him, and if he was ever in need of some personal attention, she told him to drop by. When Judy opened the door, she smiled big. Judy was a sexy, plump, dark-haired lady who loved sex.

"Hi, Judy, I'm in need of some of your personal attention."

"Well, come on in, Ben. I can help with that. I've been waiting for you to ask for a long time."

Judy was wearing just a thin silk robe, and when Ben kissed her he felt her every delicious curve. Ben didn't get home till four hours later. He was happy celebrating with Judy, and Judy was happy he came over. Sarah was still sleeping when he got home.

The next day Ben got a phone call from Mike. "Ben, I need to ask you a big favor. I have to go into the hospital for some tests, and I was wondering if you could drive me. I think they're going to keep me for a few days."

"Sure, but is it as serious as all that?"

"Well, that's what the tests will tell."

"I can pick you up today if that's early enough."

"No, I'll just come by your office."

"Okay, I'll see you then, about four?"

"Yeah, that will be fine."

Ben got tied up on an emergency phone call with another company and didn't get back to his office till 4:15. Mike was sitting across from his desk, looking worried. Mike and Ben didn't talk much on the way to the hospital.

"Mike, do they have any idea what you might have?"

"They think it could be cancer. They won't know till all the tests are done. It takes about three days."

"I didn't know it was possibly that serious."

Ben stayed with Mike as he checked in, and when he got home he broke the news to Sarah. Later Ben found Sarah quietly sobbing in the bedroom. *Let her cry for that bastard,* Ben thought. *If he kicks off I'll divorce Sarah. After all, I've already changed my will and life insurance policies, so my cheating whore wife will be without her lover or any of my money!*

After a few days Ben and Sarah went to see Mike at the hospital. Sarah kissed Mike warmly, her eyes wet.

"Mike, have you heard anything about the tests yet?" Ben asked.

"Unfortunately, yes, I have. It is cancer, and they say I have a couple of months at best to live."

The shock was evident on both Ben's and Sarah's faces. Their friend would be dead in a few short months.

"Sarah, would you excuse us for a moment? Ben and I have something to talk about."

Sarah looked questioningly at Mike and left the room.

"You fucking asshole. You found out about Sarah and me, didn't you?"

Ben was shocked. Then he smiled, like a shark smiles just before it takes a bite out of you.

"Yeah, you bastard, I found out. I came home early last month and was going to surprise Sarah by going through the back until I saw you and Sarah fucking like porn stars in the front room!"

"I thought I saw something through the sliding glass door but dismissed it as my imagination."

"Well, it was me, and it took all my willpower not to come in and bash both your skulls in!"

Mike was lying back and smiling slowly. "That was a unique form of revenge, Ben, using the St. Valentine's Day Massacre wall bricks and letting the curse work on me, but there is just one thing you didn't count on: me finding those bricks under the seat of my car! When I started feeling poorly I checked everything for hazardous waste or toxins, and imagine my surprise when I found the bricks dated 1929, the year all the gangsters were murdered."

"So, what, you found me out. In a couple of months you'll be dead, and I'll have my revenge!"

Mike laughed a bit as best he could with the tubes and IVs in him.

"What's so funny?"

"Well, old friend, when I figured out that you must have discovered Sarah was cheating on you with me, I took matters into my own hands and put one of those bricks to my own good use."

"You hid one around me? No, you're just playing with me."

"Revenge works both ways. You should make sure whomever you're seeking revenge on doesn't find out about it."

"You son of a bitch, where did you hide it?"

"Oh, now you're worried. Ha ha ha ha!"

Mike was laughing so hard he went into cardiac arrest and died right there!

Within a few days Ben made it clear to Sarah he was divorcing her, and for the next week Ben wondered where Mike could have hidden the brick. When was he alone with Mike in the last two weeks? In the car going to the hospital? No, Mike was already in his office the day Ben was late, dealing with the emergency phone call. Ben checked all through his office and desk. Nothing. Then he flipped his thickly padded chair over, and there was a slit sealed with duct tape on the bottom. Ben tore the tape off, reached inside, and pulled the brick out. He had been sitting on it all this time, and a note was taped to the brick: REVENGE WORKS BOTH WAYS, PAL! P.S. I LEFT MY LIFE INSURANCE POLICY TO SARA SO SHE WOULD BE TAKEN CARE OF. DAMN, SHE WAS GOOD IN BED!

Ben threw the brick against the wall, thinking maybe the curse wouldn't get him. He seemed to feel fine. Ben went to the restroom and washed his face with some cold water. He felt better. He went into one of the stalls and did what he had to do, but partway through, Ben was doubled over with severe cramps up into his gut. He stood up and wondered what was wrong. Then he glanced into the toilet bowl and saw that it was filled with blood. Ben knew where the cancer had gotten him and cried out in horror and pain. He ran from the restroom and jumped through a glass window! As Ben fell the ten stories to the street, he was sure that he heard Mike's laughter loud in his head.

SOOTHING THE BEAST

The night was dark and cold in Portland. Of course, that was the norm for this part of Oregon in late fall. The thing that made today especially bitter was the icy cold wind blowing at over twenty miles an hour and the fact that I was on my way to a reading of my uncle Simon's will.

My name is John, and my uncle was someone I always enjoyed visiting. Uncle Simon was a world traveler and a bit eccentric. He wasn't traditional in any sense of the word, from the way he dressed to his views on history and mythology. He would often tell me stories of mythological animals and their place in history, but after each story I would ask if what he was telling me was true. Uncle Simon would just smile and wink, saying, "What do you think, John?"

I remember the day the telegram came, notifying me of his death. He was eighty-two years old. It was a shock, since we had been so close, but a greater shock lay ahead. A few days later I received a box from his lawyers containing an old key. I was instructed to bring it to the reading of the will. As I rode to my uncle's estate in a limo furnished by his lawyers, I wondered about the brass key. While crossing a bridge, my uncle's home came into sight. It was a Victorian with several high-pointed spires overlooking the Willamette River.

I walked down the long pathway to the front door, but before I could ring the doorbell, Smith, his aide, opened the door and invited me in. "Hello, John, can I take your coat?"

"Thank you, Smith, it's good to see you again. Just wish it were under better circumstances."

Smith took me to one side. "John, your uncle wanted me to give this letter to you upon his passing and before the reading of the will."

The letter had my name on it and an unbroken wax seal.

"Did any of the others get letters like this?"

"No, you're the only one," Smith said and smiled broadly.

I opened the letter and read.

Dear John,

If you are reading this, I am dead. You need to know some things before the rest of the family reads the will. First, some members of the family want to get control of my estate. I won't let that happen, which is why I'm doing my will in this fashion. I can't give you any direct hints to solving the clues ahead of you, because it wouldn't be fair and it wouldn't be in keeping with my game-playing personality. All I can tell you is to remember our talks of history and mythology and remember you are my favorite relative.

Love,

Uncle Simon

After reading the letter, Smith led me into the den where an aunt, a stepson, a cousin, and my sister, Eileen, were. After all the introductions, we talked as Smith got us drinks. It seemed that all of us had been delivered to my uncle's home in limos and we all had keys that looked similar.

As we talked, we learned that we were the only family members who had stayed in touch with Uncle Simon all these years and knew of his eccentricities. Once we were settled, Smith brought Mr. Roberts, the lawyer, in for the first part of the will reading.

"Good evening, all of you. I'm glad you could make it, and I'm sorry for your loss," said Mr. Roberts. "Your uncle had some very specific and interesting requirements in his will. You must be able to stay here in his home until the clues are all solved, no matter how long it takes. You all must sign release forms for any injuries that might occur, releasing your uncle's estate of liability. And if any of you wish to leave now or at any time during our stay, you can and you will be given the sum of ten thousand dollars. What do all of you say?"

The only person to bail out was the stepson, Bill.

"All this fooling around by some old crazy fart isn't for me, Mr. Roberts. I'll take the ten grand and leave, thank you!"

Damn, how I wanted to punch Billy in the mouth for saying my uncle was a crazy old fart, but I bit my tongue and gripped the chair tighter and listened.

"Very well, sir. Please, come here and sign some papers, and here is your cash."

Billy's mouth fell open, seeing a banded stack of bills worth ten grand. His hand shook as he signed the papers, picked his money up, and left. We all just stared as Mr. Roberts asked if there was anyone else at this time. Nobody got up except to sign their liability forms. Then Smith led us each to our rooms, where we discovered personal belongings and clothes had been brought for our stay from each of our homes. I couldn't help thinking to myself with a smile, *Uncle, you're a crafty devil!*

The next day at breakfast we ate in the large formal dining room, and at each place setting was an envelope with our names on them. We were instructed to open them only after we reconvened in the den.

Once we opened the letters we found a small series of numbers and a letter—either a T, B, L, or R—preceding the numbers. Smith told us this was our first clue, and it would lead to the rest of the clues to solve the mystery of my uncle's will, but we should remember we must work together to solve the mystery.

Currently only my aunt Mary, sister Eileen, cousin Jim, and I were left. We decided to go to the den to study the new clues we had.

All of our keys looked just about the same, with minor differences. We examined the envelopes that we had been given to see if there was anything we missed, other than the first clue.

"May I suggest you all do your examining of the clue from the puzzle room?" Smith suggested.

The puzzle room, it turned out, was a room with a twelve-foot-high ceiling, big enough to serve as a dinner hall for fifty. At one end stood a series of ten-foot-high bookshelves and the main library, and in the middle of the room a most unique grand piano with intricate carvings, even on the keys (we found out later). Sofas and chairs occupied the area near the books. The cover of the keys to the piano had a key lock, which was unusual. We all started comparing the clues we had.

"John, do you know why Uncle would have called this his puzzle room? You knew him best of all of us." Jim said.

"Jim, I think our uncle knew that some members of our family might try to contest his will, so by setting things up this way he wouldn't have to worry about that problem, but calling this a puzzle room has got me stumped."

"Did all of you get a series of numbers and a letter?" Mary asked.

We all said yes, but we had no idea how to proceed.

"John, I once read about a code in a mystery novel, where numbers corresponded to books in a library. Could we try that, since we have this huge volume of books right here?" Eileen asked.

"Might as well, since we're right here. I don't think it's by chance that we're in this exsesively large library/den.

Eileen said she would keep a record of what we found so we could study it later. We tried my series first: L, 4, 35, 202. Because of the letter L, I started counting on the fourth row, thirty-five books in, picked the book, and turned to page 202. The page was in a book of Greek mythology, but there wasn't any other clue.

"Everyone, let me take a look at all of your keys."

Everyone passed their keys to me, and I kept them in order. There was another small difference in the keys that I had discounted as meaningless. Each key had a series of two to four spaces in different areas along the key. I got so excited my hand started to shake, and everyone was asking me if I was all right. My key had three spaces, and as I passed it down the page, only one set of three words matched up exactly: MUSIC SOOTHES DRAGONS. Everyone looked and sighed at the implication of those words. My uncle had always taught us to keep open minds. This will looked like it would test our ability to work together but to keep an open mind. When we checked all of the books against the keys, we found out that the message said: MUSIC SOOTHES DRAGONS BUT ONLY WHEN PLAYED IN THE RIGHT ORDER OR BEWARE THE DRAGONS' VENGEANCE.

We all thought about this for a while. Knowing our uncle, we could see how someone might contest his will. After we had lunch, Jim was spouting off how creepy this whole thing was.

"You can always ask Mr. Roberts to leave and get your ten thousand dollars for your trouble, Jim."

"John, I haven't given up yet, but we don't have any idea about what music our uncle was talking about. I'll give it a little more time."

We all went back to our rooms only to find another surprise. While we were eating lunch, someone had delivered small lockboxes to each of us with a new key, smaller than the one before and more delicate.

Jim was bored and couldn't sleep, so he took a walk around the estate. The more he thought to himself, the greedier he became. Why should he wait for everybody else and share the wealth of our uncle when he could try to solve the riddle himself and claim the whole thing for himself? Jim figured that a silly fool like Uncle Simon couldn't have made this treasure hunt very hard, so Jim went to the library. He noticed that a sign had been hung above the doorway: THE BLOOD ROOM. Jim smiled. *That silly old coot must have been crazy to think up these things.* He entered the room and walked to the piano, figuring any tune would solve the mystery without all the family drama, but would one of his keys unlock the piano keyboard?

Jim compared the first key with the new smaller key to the lock entrance on the grand piano. The smaller key seemed to fit. Slowly he pushed the key, his hand shaking slightly, and turned the key. The lock tumblers went free with a click, and Jim lifted the keyboard cover and pushed it into its recess. He smiled, thinking of how rich he would be, and maybe he would share a tiny bit with his family, but the lion's share would go to him because he deserved it for solving the mystery.

Since Jim didn't feel the tune mattered, he started playing "Chopsticks" on the piano from one end of the keyboard to the other. Jim waited, but nothing seemed to be happening. "That old faker, he fooled us all," Jim said out loud.

Jim started walking toward the doorway and heard movement behind him. Jim turned slowly and could not believe his eyes. His eyes widened with horror, and an earth-shattering roar filled the room. Just before he blacked out, he felt himself being lifted off the floor and shaken wildly.

Upon hearing the loud roar and door slamming, everybody came running into the hallway from upstairs. They noticed Jim wasn't there, and as they got downstairs they saw the sign above the library room.

"John, what does that mean?" Eileen asked, referring to the new sign.

"Everyone, we need to talk. Uncle Simon told me about a room in mythology called the blood room. It was used to guard huge treasures. The room would not allow anyone to get to the treasure by means of a sentry, which the designers of the room determined would make the best guard for the treasure within it."

"Smith, have you seen Jim around?"

"The last time I saw him he was headed into the blood room."

I moved toward the door and opened it, fearing the worst—that I would find my cousin Jim's body lifeless inside. We found nothing out of place, no body, all the books where we had left them, and the grand piano shut and locked in its place. We had no idea Jim had opened the grand piano at all. As we left, we noticed two items in the room, which caused goose flesh along our arms. They were both found in a planter next to the doorway. One was a tiny key to a lockbox in the dirt of the planter, and the other was a drop of blood on a green leaf that was still wet.

"We need to get out of this room and run through our clues and these new situations before we go on," I told everyone as we exited the blood room.

As we sat in the dining room, you could hear a pin drop. One of us was mysteriously gone. We hadn't opened our lockboxes yet, and we were all beginning to wonder if all of Uncle Simon's estate was worth the risk. We all decided to open our lockboxes the next morning at breakfast and sleep away the day's current events.

At breakfast, many of my relatives were silent, but we were all thinking the same thing: *Jim must be seriously injured and can't talk or he is dead!* I was trying to think about how to proceed next. The mystery was in the blood room, and that's where we would have to solve the disappearance of Jim and how he was killed or injured.

"Everyone, we need to talk out the clues, any ideas we have to solve this mystery. Uncle Simon said in a letter to me that it would take teamwork."

We started going over the clues. We had the saying given to us by Uncle Simon, but we didn't know this mystery tune that was supposed to sooth the beast, whatever it was. We were minus two people now; one took the ten grand buyout, and the other had vanished. Their boxes and keys were gone.

"Everyone, let's go outside for some air and come back to the blood room to solve the mystery."

"Sounds good to me, John," everyone said.

We walked out, and sitting on a deck chair outside was another lockbox with stepson Bill's name written on tape across the top, and it was closed. Eileen got so excited. She wondered how it got there, since Bill had left when this had all started. After picking up the box, we walked a bit, bouncing ideas off each other. Then we went back inside.

Aunt Mary spoke to our group. "How did almost all trace of violence disappear from the blood room?"

"Mary, a blood room wipes clean any evidence of intruders until the next time the sentry is disturbed," said John.

"Then why did we find the small key and the drops of blood?"

"Because the plant isn't a part of the room exactly, I believe."

We all sat near the bookshelves and opened our boxes. We all found the same small keys that Jim had found.

"Everybody, examine your box, every inch inside and out, and look for any unusual markings," I said. With an enthusiastic "Okay, John," everyone proceeded slowly. Eileen said she seemed to feel a tiny mark on her box but couldn't make it out. We went and got a magnifying lens and examined the small marks. It was a musical note. Just one! We soon found a different note on all the lockboxes but in different locations.

"We need to arrange these notes to see if we recognize the tune."

"But how can we, John? We're missing Jim's box."

"Well, if we play what we have, maybe we can solve where Jim went to."

So we moved outside the blood room doors for safety. I wrote the notes down and, since it was my idea, I would play the tune. But I didn't want to end up like Jim. I believed he was dead as soon as we found the drops of blood, but I told no one because my uncle had told me that the sentries of a blood room did not wound—they killed. And I had no intentions of being sacrificed. We enlisted the help of Smith and Mr. Roberts. Along with Eileen and Mary, they held a rope tied around my waist to haul me out of harm's way fast.

I approached the piano and slipped my small key into the lock. It felt greasy in my sweaty fingers, and I turned the key, unlocking the cover to the keys. The keys were carved with inscriptions that I could not read. I made sure my backup was ready and the line was tight, and

I began to play. When I finished, I started running, not waiting to see the sentry up close, but seeing the faces of the people at the entryway was bad enough. "Horrifying" was the only word that could describe it. As I reached the entryway, I felt hot breath at my neck, spittle hitting me in the back and an ear-deafening roar. I turned, and just before the doors slammed shut, I saw the sentry, its yellow eyes with green irises, flared nostrils, and massive black-blue scaled body. It was a dragon! I was lying in a heap at the room entrance. Everybody was asking if I was okay. I was shaking badly, and my aunt Mary (of all people) noticed I had wet my pants.

"How are we going to deal with a thing like that, John?" asked Eileen.

"I have an idea. I think we know what happened to Jim, I think he got greedy and tried the room by himself without the proper tune."

Everyone was quiet as they saw me blush when I realized that I had wet myself. Back in my room, after a shower and fresh clothes, I sat brooding over my embarrassment and wondering how my uncle Simon could have gotten such a beast as a sentry in his blood room. A knock at the door brought me out of my thoughts.

"John, are you all right?" It was my sister, Eileen.

I opened the door and told her "Sure," but not very convincingly.

"Everyone is downstairs and is very understanding. No one expected anything like what we saw. Come back downstairs, and let's solve this mystery."

"Okay."

As I joined everyone in the dining room, they all greeted me with understanding in their faces.

"John, we know what happens if you play the wrong tune. How do we figure out the right tune?" Mary asked.

"I've been thinking about that. Eileen, is it my imagination or did the tune seem familiar to you also?"

"It did, now that you mention it, but from where?"

I started to hum the tune out loud over and over. Suddenly Aunt Mary's eyes widened with recognition. "John, I know the tune. We all do. It's the one Uncle Simon used to hum to us when we were kids, to put us asleep!"

I couldn't believe it was that easy. We all made a beeline for the blood room, and I tied the safety rope back on. Mary had a good ear for music and told me what key I needed to hit for the proper note to complete the correct tune. I entered the blood room and walked to the closed piano.

My whole body was shaking, and I had broken out into a nervous sweat. Suddenly I felt two people next to me. It was Mary and Eileen.

"You two, go back in case this doesn't work."

"John, we are all in this together. Let's do this as one." Eileen said.

I was grateful for the encouragement. The three of us walked to the keys of the piano, and I unlocked it with my key.

I started to play the notes slowly so that I didn't hit a wrong key. At first nothing seemed to happen. Then the dragon reappeared but not in an agitated state. It sat before us, looking at us, and bowed its long neck so the head was but a couple of feet away from us. It let a soft growl escape its lips as it seemed to smile, the way dogs sometimes do when they are happy. Then the dragon vanished and in its place was another key and a letter.

The letter read,

Hello dearest relatives,

Since you are reading this letter you must have solved the mystery of the blood room. The key you hold will unlock my vault. Mr. Smith will show you where it is. I'm sorry for all the danger I put you through, but I needed to find out who my loyal family members were.

Thank you,

Uncle Simon

We turned to see Smith and Mr. Roberts at the entrance to the blood room, and both were smiling.

"Well, this concludes your uncle's last will and testament," Mr. Roberts said.

"Your uncle had some last words of wisdom for all of you. Use your newfound wealth wisely to help others and not just yourself," Smith said.

With that, Smith showed us to a hidden room below the old house. I used the key, we all heard the locks unlock with loud clicks, and we pulled the vault door open. It was dark until Smith flipped a side switch next to the vault entrance. All of our mouths dropped open. Within the vault were antiques from around the world, priceless pieces of history that he had collected, rare coins, and filing cabinets that we found out later were filled with stock shares and notes of all the accounts Uncle Simon had around the world. Needless to say, none of us would ever have to work again if we didn't want to.

It is three months later, and I'm thinking about how all this started with an unusual key, a limo ride, and the reading of my uncle's will. For now, Mary, Eileen, and I are going on a vacation to enjoy ourselves. It's hard to stay in touch with reality when you're riding in first class, but I've already made a decision as to what I'm going to do with my life. I'm going to follow in my uncle's footsteps, doing good where I can in the world. Maybe when my life ends I will have a blood room of my own so that my best friends and relatives can solve the mystery of soothing the beast!

THE CHAIR

The sun beat down on Pasco Prison every day, 365 days a year, making the prison a living hell. The prison was the home of the worst criminals and had a large death-row population. It's said the only way to get out of Pasco Prison was to die there. Since the sentences were so long or the inmates were executed, both options resulted in the same ending.

One inmate in particular specifically concerned the prison staff. His name was Mike Davis, and he was on death row for the multiple murders of two families. As Mike's date of execution drew closer, he got increasingly more withdrawn. Two days before his execution the guards found him in his cell, chanting gibberish and sitting inside a pentagram. When questioned, he wouldn't respond to anything asked of him.

On Mike's last day, he ate a hearty meal and created no trouble, which was very unlike Mike as an inmate. As Mike was strapped into the electric chair, he was asked if he wanted to make any statement before his sentence was carried out.

"I want to tell all of you here that I have taken measures to ensure that I will be avenged and that my evil ways will arise again in some other form." Then Mike started laughing uncontrollably.

With that, the warden gave the signal to start the execution. Mike's body started smoldering, and sparks came out of his mouth. It was the most unusual execution anyone had seen at Pasco Prison in all its history. In all, forty men had been put to death in the electric chair at Pasco, but the prison's days were numbered. Like many state agencies, due to budget cuts Pasco Prison was closed and its inmates were distributed throughout the state's other prisons. The prison itself was dismantled, and anything that could be recycled was for future use.

Five Years Later

Mark was sitting outside the conference room door, waiting for his job interview. He always hated waiting like this, as it made him feel nervous and tense. But once Mark got into the interview, everything seemed to go okay. He actually felt he had a good shot at this job with Fish and Wildlife. Mark was right. He had made a good impression on the interview panel, and they were going to call him the next day to offer him the position. But when the head of the interview panel tried to get in touch with Mark, all he got was a busy signal. Then one of the interview members brought a newspaper in to him.

"Dave, wasn't one of your job interviews yesterday with someone named Mark Jones?"

"Yes, Sherry, it was. Why do you ask?"

"It seems he made the front page of the morning paper."

Sherry handed the paper to Dave. He read an article about a young man, Mark Jones, who decided to step in front of a MAX line train in Portland just as it arrived at the stop, killing him instantly. Dave felt like he had been punched in the gut and had the wind knocked out of him. He was going to hire this promising young man yesterday.

Dave made a sympathy call to Mark's family and arranged for new interviews. Stupid HR red tape wouldn't allow them to just use the runner-up on the list. Later newspaper stories revealed some unusual circumstances surrounding Mark's death, like the fact that he had called his parents to let them know he thought he had the job and was making future plans. What the papers didn't carry was that Mark was smiling broadly when the train hit him and that the coroner noticed one side of his face had what appeared to be burn marks, possible from the friction of the side of his face meeting with the train. Both of those items were kept from the public at the request of the police.

During the next set of interviews, the person who was selected did just fine, but the runner-up didn't. Harold Menz had been trying to get any job—seasonal or full-time—and had no luck. At least this time he had a chance, or so he thought. As Harold sat in the chair outside the conference room, his hands became sweaty and he was jumpy. How was he going to remember everything he had looked up? Once the interview was over, Harold thought he did okay but wasn't sure he did his best.

When Harold received his notice in the mail that someone else had been selected, he started hearing voices in his head. *Harold, they don't want you working with them!*

My subconscious is running away with me, Harold thought to himself.

Harold, why would anybody want a loser like you?

In the space of an hour, the voices in Harold's head had convinced him that the good thing to do for everyone would be to die. Harold swallowed a bottle of sleeping pills with soda and wrote a note to anyone who cared. As Harold slipped into a sleep he would never wake from, he heard a dark hysterical laughing from a deep voice and the smell of sweat. The newspapers didn't carry simple suicides on the front page in Portland, Oregon—only the type of news that would catch people's eyes.

Dave was searching for people for seasonal employees to do some lab work, and he consulted his list of interview applicants. Harold's name came to mind, and he called the contact number. It was Harold's roommate, and he told Dave the bad news about Harold.

"What the hell is going on with our interview process? Do we need to employ mental health services to make sure we get applicants who won't kill themselves after our brutal interviews?"

No one knew what to say. For this to happen—two deaths of two interview applicants in the same department, interviewing for similar jobs—in such a few short months was unheard of. Dave contacted his friend with the Portland Police, Detective Johnson.

"Hey, Dale, how have you been?"

"Just fine, Dave, what's on your mind?"

"Well, something's bothering me. It seems we had two of our applicants interviewing for similar jobs in my department commit suicide within a couple months of each other. It seems like a whale of a coincidence."

"Give me their names and I'll look into it for you. I didn't know your interviews for state jobs were so tough."

"This isn't funny. They were both young people with a lot to live for, so I would like to get some answers if possible."

"Okay, sorry, I'll find out whatever I can."

It was a few days before Dave heard back from Dale, and Dale was acting more like a cop than a friend when he called him back.

"Dave, why are you so interested in these suicides?"

"I told you, it seemed like too much of a coincidence for two people committing suicide while applying for jobs in the same department."

"Well, there were a couple things that were kept out of the papers by the police." Dale told Dave about the unusual aspects of Mark's death, and Dave was shocked.

"Dale, do you think this warrants more looking into?"

"Yes, it does seem weird, and given what little we know, I would like to do the checking on this if that's okay."

"Sure, that would be great. If you need help let me know."

Dale began his investigation quietly and looked into both backgrounds. He even found out from Harold's roommate that Harold had been hearing voices, a fact the other detectives hadn't been made aware of. So far Dale could only find that both people went to interviews at the same place and nothing else. One of Dave's friends at work, Karen, asked if she could borrow a chair for their interviews, and Dave went ahead and loaned the one he usually used outside the conference room. Karen brought the chair back and announced that she had a person who smoked the interview and it couldn't have gone better.

The next day, as Dave worked at his desk, he suddenly heard gunshots in the compound. Outside he saw a young man firing a pistol randomly at people through the windows of buildings. Sirens were already coming down the hill from a 911 call, and a cop on a megaphone told everyone to stay inside till they could clear the area.

When all was said and done, luckily only one person had been shot and none killed. The weirdest thing was that the shooter was the person Karen had selected for the job, and she had already told him the good news. So why had he gone on a rampage? Dave talked with Dale in private a bit.

"Dave, this area out here is getting lousy with crime. Can you tell me anything that might help?"

"The only things that tie them together are the fact that they were looking for jobs and Karen, the head of the interview board, borrowed our interview chair."

Just then both Dale and Dave got an expression on their faces like they had just swallowed something gross.

"Let's have a look at this everyday chair you use for your waiting job applicants."

Dale and Dave found the chair easy enough. It had a nondescript formed frame and a blue fabric back and seat.

"Dave, when the state buys cheap, they go all the way."

"Yeah, Dale, they do what comes naturally."

As they examined the cheap chair, Karen walked by.

"Be careful, one of our new hires, Collen Bradford, got a nasty cut from one of the edges of that chair."

Dale and Dave started examining every inch of the chair. They found a curved piece of metal bent away from the frame, sharp as a razor, but the unusual thing was when Dale shined his pocket light on the area it revealed a serial number stamped into the metal.

"Dale, can you trace that number?"

"I think I can. If I can't, the FBI can."

It took Dale two days to get the results of tracing the chair's serial number. When he read the results and questioned the chair maker a bit more, he got strangely excited and called Dave.

"You aren't going to believe what I found out about your common interview chair. It seems the chair was made out of recycled materials by a company that won a bid on a big recycling job."

"What kind of job was it?"

"It was Pasco Prison. After it was closed, the company won the bid to recycle everything in the prison that was worth anything, including the item with the serial number."

"Dale, what item did the serial number match?"

"It matched the electric chair they used at the prison."

There was dead silence between both men for a minute.

"Dale, are you trying to tell me that somehow our chair we use for interviews is causing people to go off the deep end because it was part of an electric chair?"

"I think we better investigate the backgrounds of the people who went off the deep end and cross-check it with the inmates who rode Old Sparky to their death."

"Okay, but I want this to be kept just between you and me until we have solid evidence."

"Okay, Dave, I'll keep in touch."

Dave put the chair away in a storage room and locked it up. The next time he talked to Dale was on the phone.

"Dave, can you meet me tomorrow at 9:00 a.m. at my home?"

"Sure, but why?"

"I've got something to show you, and I'd rather not talk on the phone about it, okay?"

"Okay, I'll see you at 9:00 a.m."

When Dave got to Dale's home the next morning, he was greeted warmly by Dale.

"Dave, I hope you're ready for a full day of weirdness."

"Dale, why do you say that?"

Dale smiled and brought out a huge folder file. "This is the result of my investigation of your common chair, Dave."

Dale explained that Pasco Prison was where the most violent criminals were sent. And there was a list of all the inmates on death row who had been executed, forty in all. But only one of the interviewees had any relationship to a death-row inmate. Her name was Colleen Bradford.

"Dale, there's no Bradford on the execution list."

"That's her mom's maiden name. Her married name was Davis."

"So Colleen is really Mike Davis's daughter, the last man executed at Pasco Prison!"

"Can we talk to Colleen's mom and ask her a few questions?"

"Sure, I already made an appointment. She knows we're coming."

They arrived at a small home, and Betty Bradford let them in.

"Mrs. Bradford, we don't mean to upset you, but we would like to ask you a few questions about your husband, Mike Davis."

"Why would you want to ask about him? I've kept Colleen shielded from what her father did all her life."

"Mrs. Bradford, our investigation of some erratic behavior has been traced back to your husband and his stay at Pasco Prison."

"All I have of that period in my life is what the prison sent me as his last personal effects when he died. I haven't even opened the box."

"May we look into that box?"

Betty thought for a moment and then tearfully nodded yes. As Dale and Dave started going through the items in the box, a letter addressed to Colleen and Betty fell out of a shirt pocket. On the front was printed: TO BE READ AFTER MY DEATH. The letter was still sealed, so Dale carefully opened it. Inside Mike told his wife and daughter how much he loved them and that the hellish prison he was in had forced him to try to get vengeance on the prison staff in what might be considered a crazy fashion. It seems Mike had found in the prison library a book of Hindu curses, so the gibberish Mike was speaking was this curse. It would, in effect, turn the instrument of his death on those around him. Mike could never have guessed he would be the last person electrocuted at Pasco, and then the prison would be scrapped. Somehow the curse got warped when the chair was made, so anyone who was not his blood relative would go crazy with violence to others and or themselves.

Both Dave and Dale took a few days off to fathom what they had found out about the chair. They also brought the chair to a metal smelter and watched as it dissolved into angry orange molten metal to be formed into something else, but hopefully the curse would be gone.

THE DRAG RACE

Jake and Mary were parked in Jake's Mustang on a deserted road. Mary loved making out with Jake. His rough hands all over her body seemed to make sex all the better. Before long, Jake and Mary were naked, and Jake was making love to her, though most would have called it lust, not love, a more descriptive term of what they were doing. Jake was powerful, forceful, and never considered Mary's pleasure or feelings. He had even kicked her out of the car a couple of times, making her walk back a couple of times. Jake was a creep and a bully, and Mary didn't know why she stayed with him.

To go back to Mary's place, they drove down Main Street. The car next to Jake, a Camaro, gunned its engine. When the light at the intersection turned green, both cars started off at high speed, racing each other. They reached over eighty miles per hour by the time the race was done. Jake had lost by a foot.

"God damn it, Mary, this is your fault!"

"How do you figure?"

"If you weren't in the car, my car would have been lighter and I would have won!"

Mary started to cry. "How could you say that, Jake, after just having sex with me? I thought you cared!"

"You're nothing special. I could have sex with any girl I wanted. After all, I'm a Demon and we get anything we want when we want it!"

The Demons were the gang Jake belonged to, and they had had a few close calls with the Portland Police about drag racing and booze.

Mary got out of Jake's car and slammed the door.

"Take it easy on my car, Mary!" Jake yelled.

"Fuck you, Jake, I'm tired of being used and abused. Stay away from me, asshole!"

"Oh, you'll come back. You love what Jake's packing."

"But I don't like how it's packaged, Jake!"

Mary walked home as Jake peeled out for his own place.

Jake stopped by the Demons' clubhouse the next day. Word had spread that Jake had lost the race on Main Street.

"Hey, Jake, you losing your touch?" asked his friend Mike as he grinned.

"Hell no, Mike. Just had some deadweight in my car, my girlfriend."

They all started laughing at that.

"That's why when I'm looking to get some from my girl, I take her to a no-tell motel, screw her brains out, and take her home. That way if someone challenges me to a drag, it's just me and my car," Bob said.

They all agreed that was a much better idea. After all, they were Demons and they had a reputation to uphold with winning races and girls—in that order.

The next day Jake put in a token appearance at his high school. Normally he avoided school, and most of the teachers in the school considered him a lost cause. Even his drunken parents couldn't care less if Jake went to school. But today was different. Since Mary had dumped him, he needed a new girlfriend to satisfy his animal lust, someone who would look up to him, until she got tired of being used.

There was no shortage of girls who would have liked to be with Jake due to his bad-boy nature and reputation. After all, he was a Demon! Actually, girls weren't the only thing on Jake's mind. The big citywide drag races started in two months. The races were held at an official drag strip, and there was even prize money for the top racer in each classification. Jake wanted to win top eliminator in his category and the ten grand that went with it. He headed for the Demons club in the afternoon to make plans for the races and to pick out his new girlfriend.

God has a wry sense of humor. He can make angels of any soul, whether they are in heaven or on earth. In the case of the Angel of Death, God selected a person's soul who exhibited the darkest nature of humans and gave him the job. He gathered souls from earth and guided them, as God directed Heaven or Hell. God came to the Angel of Death one day long ago and told him he had earned the right to enter Heaven as soon as Death found a proper replacement. Death had been looking for hundreds of years for the right person.

Jake had decided to fine-tune his car by racing in every official drag race he could find to build up points toward being top eliminator in his classification. And Jake was very successful, so much so that he started to become more boastful and arrogant about his skills in a car.

At one evening race, after winning his last match for the night, Jake and a few buddies were walking through the pits as he bumped hard into a guy with his back turned. Most normal people would have apologized but not Jake. "Hey, dumb fuck, watch where you're going!" Jake yelled.

"I think you bumped into me, sir," the stranger said in a calm voice.

"It was your fault for standing in my way."

Grinning to himself, the stranger let Jake see his smile of contempt for him and turned his back on him.

"Hey, if you had a car I'd wipe that stupid grin off your face."

The stranger slowly turned, still grinning. "I do have a car. It's right over there."

Jake turned and looked where they had just passed. There sat a black 1968 Ford Mustang Fastback, gleaming in the dark with a black interior. Jake didn't remember passing that car and would have sworn it wasn't there a moment ago. Jake said nothing.

"Are you really as good as you say you are, sir?"

"Damn straight!"

"Well, then, why don't we settle this at the drag races later this month, winner takes all."

"You're on. I hope you're ready to lose your car. I might be able to sell that old piece of crap for parts."

The stranger smiled and added as he passed Jake, "It's winner takes all!"

Jake watched the stranger get into his car and start the engine, possibly to get an idea of what he had under the hood. But when the car started and the exhaust could be seen in the cool night air, the car was quiet as a mouse, even when the stranger drove off, still grinning at him. The hairs on Jake's neck prickled for some reason, and as Jake got ready to drive off, he couldn't relax at all. He was spooked. All night Jake kept trying to imagine what engine the guy had that was that quiet. He was familiar with most engines, but none were that quiet—not high-performance cars.

Jake never saw the stranger after that night, at least not up close. Sometimes he thought he caught a glimpse of him in a crowd, or his black Mustang following him, but it never proved out. Jake couldn't figure out why the stranger bugged him so much or why he reminded Jake that their race would be winner takes all. The next time Jake saw the stranger for sure was at the statewide drag races. All the racers were going through their elimination rounds, leading to the top eliminator in each classification, and it looked like the stranger was racing in Jake's class. The stranger and Jake raced all comers until it was just the two of them.

"Hey, stranger, get ready to have your ass handed to you!" Jake yelled across the drag strip.

The stranger just gave Jake a wide toothy grin, his teeth shining with moisture. Both cars began staging up to the starting line, engines revving up, though Jake's was incredibly louder. The evening was lit up with the racing lights. The Christmas tree ran through its lights. When it hit green, both drivers blasted off, smoke pouring off their rear tires.

A third of the way down the track, Jake looked over at the stranger's car and suffered what could only be a shocking waking dream. He saw the driver dressed in a hooded cloak, and in the hood of the cloak was a gleaming white skull staring right at him. The vision only lasted a few seconds, but it distracted Jake enough. Fire roared from under the Mustang as it shot forward, easily passing Jake and crossing the finish line first. Jake was out of his car in an instant.

"You fuck, you cheated and used some illegal equipment. I demand that the race officials look under your hood!"

The officials asked if they could look at the stranger's engine.

"By all means, go right ahead."

The stranger leaned against his car, and Jake watched him. It was then that Jake realized that the stranger was dressed all in black from head to toe. The official turned to Jake and announced that there was

85

nothing illegal about the Mustang's 289 V8. Jake was so dumbfounded that his mouth fell agape. The stranger approached Jake and asked him if he would be more comfortable concluding their business at his home. Jake just shook his head and gave the stranger his address.

The stranger arrived at Jake's home and was let in. His parents were passed out in their bedroom.

"Well, here is the pink slip to my car, bastard!"

The stranger smiled. "Jake, did you forget this was a winner-takes-all race?"

"You have all I can give. What more do you want?"

"Jake, I want your soul. I've been waiting for hundreds of years to find someone with the right attitude to train."

"Train to do what?"

"To become the next Angel of Death."

"But I would have to be dead. I'm too young to die!"

The stranger just smiled, his voice low but menacing. "Someone like you would serve better as my apprentice than living a full life here."

"I'm not going anywhere with you."

Again, Death just laughed, showing his true form, a skeleton dressed in a hooded black cloak. As Jake started backing away, Death extended his arm, pointing his finger at Jake. There was a blue-black flash, and Jake seemed to be looking down on his living room with him sitting in a chair. People were moving around the room. Jake heard one of the people comment about him.

"Even with all the stories I've heard about this guy, he at least did one decent thing. He left a brief will, giving his car to his former girlfriend that he abused so she would have enough money to start to go to college."

"I never wrote anything like that for that bitch. What do I care if she goes to college!"

"Jake, I thought it would be a nice gesture, seeing how it will be your last."

Just then Jake saw a person enter the room and read what was on the back of his coat. Jake screamed.

"Come now, Jake, there is much I have to teach you."

As Death pulled Jake away to learn his new trade, the vision of the word on the guy's coat kept revolving in his eyes: MORGUE!

THE SECRET

The rain was coming down hard as Brian got into his car to go to work. As he drove out of the West Hills into town he was reminded of just how much he loved his car, a new sleek black Jag. What Brian didn't like was the cold weather that accompanied the rain in Portland, Oregon. When it got cold, the scar on his left shoulder ached intensely. The only thing that helped was an ointment the doctor had given him, and the fact that the person that wounded him was behind bars. Who would've thought a mild-mannered wife could be such a vicious bitch!

As Brian rode the elevator up to his office in the bank building, it stopped and a very curvaceous, attractive woman got on. Brian knew where she was going. It was his assistant, Gina. She smiled. "How's it going, Brian?" Gina asked.

"It's wet, cold, but otherwise okay," Brian told her.

As they got off at their floor, Gina rubbed up against Brian, licking her lips. She smiled and walked away. Brian enjoyed the view of Gina walking away. She was such a flirt, and Brian knew she wanted to go out with him. Someday, maybe. Brian turned and went into his office. It was large with floor-to-ceiling windows on one side that overlooked the city of Portland and the Willamette River. Brian took off his shirt and applied some ointment to his shoulder wound before he began his work. *Aaaah!*

As Ann sat in her cell, she grew more and more depressed, and the steady rain outside wasn't helping her mood. A guard approached. It was Thompson.

"Are you feeling down, hon?" the guard asked in a sarcastic tone. The guard unlocked the cell door. "Someone wants to have a private conversation with the crazy lady, so get a move on."

Thompson nudged her with his nightstick. An evening visit like this could mean big trouble, the kind that put you in the infirmary for a while. They walked to a corridor where they had group counseling rooms; Ann was let into one of them. The room was dark and smelled of the new plastic chairs that they sat on.

"Is anyone here?" Ann asked.

Ann's heart was thudding in her chest when suddenly she heard footsteps moving toward her, and a voice. "Don't worry, Ann, I'm a friend."

The person approached, and Ann recognized the voice and the faint smell of perfume. It was Beth.

"Why all the secrecy, Beth?" Ann asked.

"Well, I wasn't sure how you would react after I talked to you."

"I care about you, Ann, very much," Beth said.

Ann was quiet, but when Beth took her hand gently, her anxiety grew.

"Beth, I haven't experienced these types of feelings from another woman. I'm not sure . . ."

But Beth hushed Ann gently and comforted her. Ann couldn't believe how wonderful she was feeling in Beth's arms, as time seemed to slip by too rapidly. Ann and Beth were led back to their cells, and for the first time in a long while, Ann slept peacefully.

Brian received a rather harsh phone call while at work. The caller was one of Brian's clients whom he dealt with in his extracurricular activities. The client, a Mr. Zim, was upset at Brian's inability to fill his order.

"Now, now, Mr. Zim, I assure you I can meet all of your needs," Brian assured.

"You had better do it right. All I've been doing is waiting on you, and then when you do deliver the quality is at times poor," Mr. Zim yelled.

"If you don't shape up, Brian, I'm going to talk to your boss." *Click.*

Brian had heard the phone click but still held the phone, cursing under his breath. How dare that butthead threaten him! It was then that Brian noticed he had broken out in a massive body sweat. He was drenched. Brian decided to change into casual clothes and leave before he met Mr. Zim.

By the time Brian had run his errands and picked up the package for Mr. Zim, he had an hour left before his meeting, just enough time to get there. As Brian pulled up in front of Zim's warehouse, Mr. Zim's limo rounded the corner. No one saw them because the warehouse district was deserted this time of night. The black limo stopped in front of Brian, and a window came down. The smell coming from inside the limo was putrid and vile. The inside of the car was completely black.

"Brian, did you bring me my order?"

"Most definitely, Mr. Zim. I think you will be very happy with your order."

A gnarled hand shot out, grabbing Brian and pulling him toward the limo's dark window. "I hope so for your sake, Brian." Then Brian was flung backward toward his own car. "Let me inspect my package."

Brian unzipped the bag, exposing the contents. Mr. Zim leaned out of the open window into the glow of a nearby streetlight. Every time Brian saw Mr. Zim in the light, the nickname "butthead" seemed more fitting. Mr. Zim's head had a cleft from the top of his head to his nasal passage, his head was bulbous and without hair, and there was a series of wavy ridges extending down from his glowing yellow eyes to the lips of his mouth, which was full of needlelike teeth. Mr. Zim also had the right attitude for the nickname.

Inside the bag was an attractive unconscious woman in her midtwenties.

"Brian, I told you a blonde. This a redhead!"

"But, Mr. Zim, nobody told me of that requirement."

Mr. Zim turned toward his assistant and, picking him up, folded him in half backward, snapping his back. Mr. Zim threw the body of his assistant into the trash, as if nothing had happened.

"Brian, I may be able to sell this one as a servant to one of my friends, but I won't keep her," Mr. Zim said.

"If you don't mind me asking, why do you favor blondes?"

"I have found that blondes have the most wonderfully delicious screams of terror of any human females."

"Well, I aim to please, Mr. Zim. I will have your order filled promptly by Friday."

"That soon? You must already have someone in mind. That would be excellent!"

Mr. Zim offered his hand/claw to Brian, who shook it, but neither hand looked very human. Brian drove his car home, satisfied that Mr. Zim's requirements would be met soon. He was right. Brian did have a young blonde in mind who would be perfect.

Ann's daily routine was pretty boring until today, when Beth introduced her to Belinda Langusti. Belinda's hubby was accused of having mob connections, although it was never proven. Belinda was accused of laundering the mob money through her small business, and in prison awaiting trial. When Belinda was arrested she was offered a deal if she would rat out her husband, but she refused and ended up here.

Belinda, Ann, and Beth talked for a long while. Finally, Belinda asked Ann and Beth how they would like to get out of here.

"How?" Ann asked.

"My husband, Tony, isn't happy I'm here and wants me out right now, any way possible," Belinda said.

Both Ann and Beth said they were in.

Ann felt this may be the chance she'd been waiting for to expose Brian, but she needed to talk to her brother, the priest, when he visited tomorrow.

Belinda told Ann and Beth to be ready in three days, Friday, and to volunteer for extra laundry duty on the first shift. Both Ann and Beth did as they were told. As they returned to their cells, anticipation had all three inmates thinking of the future.

On Wednesday Ann's brother, Mike, came to visit. Ann requested a quiet room for the visit. These rooms were the ones guards could watch but not hear what was being said. They were used in special instances for meetings with lawyers or to receive bad news.

When Ann spoke to her brother she let it all out as to why she stabbed Brian and everything leading up to it.

"That's a fantastic story, sis, but what do you want me to do?"

"Mike, first, do you believe me?"

"Well, it would explain why they sealed your statement and put you in here instead of in the general prison population. Yeah, I guess I believe you."

"And second, Brian needs to be exposed, if not stopped altogether. How would I do that?"

"Well, as your brother I believe you, but as a priest I can't allow myself, as a church representative, to accept your story. However, if we were speaking hypothetically, there are many weapons that can be used against evil or demonic entities, anything that has been blessed."

"So, if a person brought you some items to be blessed—no questions asked—hypothetically that would work?"

"Sure, sis. Let me know if I can do anything for you."

"I'll keep that in mind."

Ann and her brother hugged. As she was close to him she whispered, "Stay at home Friday all day, okay?"

Mike looked at her for a long time and then nodded.

As Brian worked Wednesday, his assistant seemed intent on using every chance to brush up against him or entice him verbally. Now, Brian was a bit of an oddity among his particular group, because he enjoyed the physical encounters with human females. And since his wife had gone to prison, he had had many opportunities for such encounters with the ladies he worked with regularly. But Gina, his assistant, was becoming annoying to the extreme, so Brian decided to take matters into his own hands.

At the end of the workday, Brian and Gina shared an elevator down. Brian asked her if she would like to have a drink after work. Her face cracked into the biggest smile. Brian knew the answer before she spoke.

Brian and Gina went to a local bar, got a booth in the back, and ordered. After some shoptalk and gossip, Gina snuggled close to Brian. This would have normally been good for Brian, but because she was so shallow and pushy, Brian could only think about what a loathsome creature she was—as ugly on the inside as Mr. Zim was on the outside. It made his skin crawl.

Soon Brian and Gina were deeply kissing and caressing each other. Gina whispered, "Let's go to my place."

"Okay," Brian agreed.

They entered Gina's apartment on the twentieth floor after a short drive. As the door shut, Brian pressed Gina against the wall and pulled her tightly to him as he deeply kissed her again. Gina moved from Brian as she unbuttoned the top of her blouse, moving toward the dining room table. Brian followed right behind her, acting more like a hunter than a lust-filled lover.

"Let me get out of my work clothes, okay, Brian?" Gina said.

Instead of answering right away, Brian pressed up against her from behind, pulling her close and holding her by the hips.

"Brian, your lust is showing," she said as she pushed back into him.

Brian started squeezing and pinching Gina, who noticed Brian's voice had become wet and raspy. Brian kissed Gina's neck and back.

"Let me turn around so I can see your face," Gina said.

"Is that what you really want?"

"Yes."

Gina started to turn her head, and Brian leaned closer. When Gina saw his face, horror filled her eyes. Suddenly Brian grabbed her head and, with a quick twist, snapped her neck! A look of surprise and terror on her face, Gina was looking backward into Brian's face, even though the rest of her body faced forward. Brian smiled and thought, *There you go, Gina dear, just what you wanted, to look at my face.*

On Thursday Brian came to work early because he had an early dinner date with Claire, a young blonde office assistant who readily agreed to his dinner invitation. Suddenly, there was a loud commotion out in the hallway. Brian got out from behind his desk and stared out his office windows at the city. A coworker burst in.

"Someone has murdered Gina. It's in the morning newspaper, and they say it was grotesque but didn't give any details."

"Have some flowers sent from me as soon as you can, purple roses."

"Okay, boss," the coworker said as he wrote everything down. As he left the office he couldn't see the smug smile frozen on Brian's face and the cheerful gleam in his eyes.

Brian met with Claire at a local restaurant near their office. The food and atmosphere were both very good. Brian enjoyed being with Claire, because she was not only beautiful but smart too. Brian thought about this as he laced Claire's drink with a special drug while she was away from the table. Mr. Zim would be very pleased with Claire.

When Brian and Claire left, Claire got dizzy, so Brian offered to drive her home. Just as they got to Brian's car, Claire passed out, although her eyes were still open. Brian just smiled as he stuffed Claire's body into the canvas bag and drove off to meet Mr. Zim.

Mr. Zim's limo was waiting at his warehouse as Brian arrived. Brian pulled up alongside the limo, got out, and popped the trunk on the Jag.

"Did you fill my order?" Mr. Zim asked through the limo window.

"Let me show you," Brian said with a smile.

Brian removed the canvas bag from the trunk and laid it near the limo. He then unzipped it, revealing a semi-alert Claire, eyes open but unable to move or speak.

"Oh, Brian, she's excellent." Mr. Zim ran one clawed hand through Claire's blonde hair.

All Claire was aware of was that she wanted to scream her lungs out and run away from the two nightmarish figures that stood over her, but she seemed paralyzed. *Damn you, Brian!* As Mr. Zim's new assistant loaded the bag containing Claire into the trunk of the limo, Brian and Mr. Zim concluded their transaction.

"Brian, you have outdone yourself. I think you deserve a bonus," Mr. Zim told Brian as he handed him a manila envelope. "There's 100K in there with an extra 20K for your outstanding effort."

"Thank you very much, Mr. Zim. If I can be of help in the future, please let me know."

"Oh, I will. I can hardly wait to get her home and hear how wonderfully she screams!"

Brian had noticed as Mr. Zim spoke that his voice became throaty and wet, almost like he was drooling as he spoke.

"Have a nice evening, Mr. Zim," Brian said as the limo started to pull away.

"I will!"

And Brian heard Mr. Zim laughing out loud until the limo window closed all the way. As Brian reached his home in the West Hills he smiled to himself about a profitable night and another satisfied customer.

On Friday morning at 5:00 a.m., Belinda, Beth, and Ann all arrived on time for the first laundry shift with the help of the guards. Outside, a laundry van pulled up to the loading dock. Ann saw the driver wink at Belinda and get out to unload the fresh linen. As the dirty linen was being loaded, the three women casually walked into the back of the van as the guard did his crossword puzzle. All three women disappeared from sight. The driver got ready to leave when Thompson, the guard, asked where the women were.

"I think one of the other guards took them back to their cells," the driver told him.

The van took off through the prison gate, never to be seen again. The Langusti residence was actually a walled estate, made very private with the high-tech security that had been installed. The van had dropped the ladies off at the front door after releasing them from the hidden floor panel. Then the driver, Belinda's brother Steve, hugged his sister and took the van to make it disappear.

After Belinda and Tony hugged and kissed a lot, introductions were made.

"Any friends of my wife must be good people. If you need anything just ask," Tony said.

"Well, Mr. Langusti, we could use a car," Ann said.

"Please call me Tony, and go right ahead and use any one you like. Just phone me to let me know where to pick it up, okay?"

"Thank you, Tony."

Belinda led Ann and Beth to a large underground garage. Ann picked out a dark green '99 Taurus SE that would blend right in with traffic. They all said their good-byes and left. Ann decided to drive.

"Where are we going, Ann?"

"To my brother Mike's church first."

Portland had many large churches, but Ann's brother's church was a small one located in Southeast Portland. When they arrived they went to the priest's quarters and Mike answered the door.

"I thought you might be dropping by, Ann, especially after what I saw on the news."

"What do you mean?"

Mike showed both women into the living room, where a TV broadcast was in progress about a riot at a minimum-security prison.

"It seems some of your roommates didn't like being left behind and are rioting. They say over a 100 have escaped of the 1100-prisoner population."

"Mike, can you help us with some special weapons?" Ann changed the focus of the conversation.

Mike smiled. "I've already put some things together for you."

Mike opened a velvet bag and revealed two silver letter openers, a vial of holy water, and a sacramental ribbon priests use at mass. He blessed the objects in Latin and carefully instructed Ann and Beth on how to use them.

"These work best if you can surprise the subject you're using them on," Mike said.

Ann and Beth arrived at Brian's house just after dark. They prepared the weapons as Mike had instructed, by pouring holy water over the blades of the letter openers. Then Ann had Beth wrap the sacramental ribbon around the handle of Beth's letter opener. The only key Ann still had to this home was to a side door. They entered through the door using Ann's key, and Ann went upstairs to look around while Beth hid downstairs. As Ann entered what used to be their bedroom, she noticed a day planner on the table next to the bed. She leafed through it and stared with disbelief. In the planner were names, dates, and payment amounts. Also two columns jumped out at her with check marks designating "soul" or "servant." As Ann read and realized what Brian had been dealing in, she heard a car pull into the driveway.

Brian shut his car door and walked to the house. Once inside he went first to the kitchen and then to the den. After making a fire in the fireplace, Brian sat back, reflecting on his good fortune. Today he had made a $120,000 deposit and had a very special call from his supervisor of his extracurricular activities. Mr. D. had called Brian at the bank, which seldom occurred.

"Brian, Mr. Zim contacted me a while ago, wanting to let me know how well you did with his order," Mr. D. said.

"I'm pleased Mr. Zim was happy, Mr. D."

"He was more than happy. He was pleasantly exhausted and said to tell you that she was delicious."

Both Brian and Mr. D. laughed hard at that.

"Brian, if you keep up this quality of work, I would like to offer you the Pacific Northwest supervisor position."

Brian's mouth fell open as he took the good news in.

"But, Mr. D., isn't that your position?"

"*Was*. They're moving me up the ladder and asked me to recommend someone. What do you say?"

"Why yes, sir. I'd be honored."

"Good. After all, we have to control these humans."

With that, Mr. D. ended the conversation and Brian left work in order to have an expensive dinner and several drinks to celebrate.

As Brian sat in the den, he surfed the TV channels and got a local news program. They were covering a prison riot with escaped prisoners. As Brian listened, he realized that the riot was at the prison where Ann was.

Ann grabbed the day planner and quietly walked along the dark upstairs hallway toward the stairs. She could hear the TV and saw the flickering light reflected off the walls from the fireplace. As Ann moved, she accidentally scraped the molding at the base of the wall.

"Damn it!" Ann said.

Brian heard the noise and muted the TV. He listened for a few minutes and then called out, "Whoever you are, you have picked the worst possible place to rob!"

At first the only answer was the wind outside.

Then in a calm, low voice, Ann responded, "Oh, I think I have the right place!"

Ann made her way along the hallway to the steps as Brian got up and stared out the entry to the den.

"Well, well, you silly bitch, why have you come back?" Brian jeered.

Brian made his way back to the chair near the fireplace. After all, it was only his stupid wife, and she wasn't any threat to him. Ann entered the den cautiously, taking in her surroundings.

"I came back to tie up some loose ends, Brian!"

"I've just been watching some of your cell mates at the loony bin trash the place. Seems like they didn't like being left behind."

Ann just smiled and fondled the day planner. Brian's face lost its smugness.

"This is a very interesting book you have. I bet the cops would love to go over it with you, especially the columns marked 'soul' and 'servant.'" Ann spoke with confidence.

Brian went to get up but stopped when Ann pulled the silver letter opener out from its hiding place.

"Do you think something like that can do me serious damage, Ann?"

"Do you know what you put me through? You haven't lived till you've sampled the great psychotic cocktails they served up in that hellhole!"

Brian laughed harder and his voice got raspy and wet-sounding. "I've always wondered one thing. Why did you stab me in the first place?"

"One day I saw you near the mirror in our bedroom. I doubt you even knew I was there, but I saw what you really look like, Brian, and I had to bite my tongue to keep from screaming out loud."

"Guess I just got a bit careless."

"But no matter. I'll just have to get rid of you. Maybe I'll sell you to one of my clients as a plaything."

"Well, why don't you show me your real self now, since we're being open about things?"

Before Ann finished speaking, Brian's features had dramatically changed. His face was crimson red but pale and covered with large brown spots, like moles with coarse-looking hair growing from them. Brian's nose wasn't really a nose, as we know it, but a pair of open wet sinus passages with bony ridges above it that decreased in width as they went up to his eyes. And those eyes—black pupils that looked like you could fall into them and never hit bottom, surrounded by deep yellow with tiny red veins running throughout, like he had bloodshot eyes all the time. It was horrible to look at Brian's true image, but Ann forced herself to stare.

"Is this what you wanted, Ann?"

"Much better. This way I can kill you easier without thinking of the man I fell in love with."

Brian smiled, revealing pointed yellow teeth that curved inward slightly, and he laughed—so hard, as a matter of fact, that Ann noticed his gross tongue slide across his lips, pink with black spots. Ann's stomach rolled as she saw this and turned away for a second.

"My dear Ann, how can you kill me when you can't even stand to look at me?"

Ann looked right into Brian's eyes, thinking of all the hell she had been through because of Brian, and her gaze didn't waver. Brian stopped smiling at once.

"I think I will sell you to one of my clients. He likes to have new playthings for dinner, literally!"

At that, Ann's rage couldn't be held back. "You aren't going to make me part of your perverted business!"

Ann was only about six feet away from Brian as she threw the letter opener. The firelight glinted off the silver blade as it flew through the air and glanced off Brian's upper left arm.

"Damn it!" Ann shouted.

"You bitch! What have you done to me? It stings and burns!" Brian cried out in rage.

Ann smiled as she saw Brian's gnarled hand go to his wound, which for some reason was not only bleeding but small wisps of steam were coming from it. When Brian removed his hand, it was covered with an orange goo right down to the clawlike fingernails, and the room started to smell a bit like burning tires.

"Fuck my customer! I'm going to rip your body apart for this!"

Brian went to get up, but suddenly from behind he heard a scream somewhere between rage and insanity: Beth. Brian felt the other letter opener jam hard into his ribs as he roared in pain and horror. He turned to his side and saw the letter opener jammed to the hilt in his ribs. Then he noticed that the handle was wrapped in a priest's sacramental ribbon. Brian swung a clawed hand at Beth but missed.

Ann walked up to Brian, who had collapsed back in his chair. Something was happening to his body. Brian realized he was mortally wounded.

"You must have talked to that bastard brother of yours, Ann. You couldn't have figured all this out on your own."

Ann smiled as she noticed more orange goo leaking from Brian's lips and nostrils. His body was falling apart and dissolving into a puddle. Ann went to Brian's desk and found the hidden key Brian kept for the top left-hand drawer of the desk and used it. Searching briefly, she came upon what she needed: a small leather-covered notebook with account numbers at several local banks.

"Brian, let me introduce you to my friend Beth," Ann said.

Beth smiled and said nothing.

"I want to thank you, Brian, for keeping my name on all the accounts. I guess it was a good way for you to keep up the caring husband illusion.

The money from these accounts will mean a new start for Beth and me."

Brian's body was quickly collapsing in on itself as Brian realized his end was near.

"I hope you burn in hell, Ann—you and your bitch!" Brian managed to say.

"Maybe, but you go first. If we see you there, fine. But if we don't, well, hon, you just cherish this memory of how I got even with you and this." Ann turned and kissed Beth deeply on the mouth. "I hope it keeps you nice and warm!"

Ann and Beth looked at Brian and laughed together as Brian died, his mouth agape. Just then a pitch pocket exploded from the fireplace, showering the carpet with hot coals that started to burn.

"Beth, let's get going and look for our new place to live," Ann said.

By the time Ann and Beth pulled out of the driveway, the den was fully in flames. Ann saw the light from the burning home in the rearview mirror. Some say it's not good to look back, but in this instance it was good. *Very* good.

THE SINGER

My name is Mike James, and the first time I met Syrus Gupp was on my first day at Johnson State Prison. I was a new member of the staff. Having just completed my training the previous summer, I was lucky to be appointed to a maximum-security prison, like Johnson. Syrus was a plain sort of man, a stereotype of a civil servant. He dressed plainly in a dark-colored suite and tie, and he was very quiet. The most striking thing about him was his neck; it was badly scarred along the front with the scars running up to above where his voice box would be. The white lines of the scars stood out like veins on his neck. Syrus never talked to me about how he got the scars, but I eventually found out.

Syrus had been coming home from a party as a teenager when he hit a slick spot on the road and hit a tree. One of the branches was thrown through the windshield of his car, and the glass struck him in the throat. Luckily the doctors saved his voice, but soon Syrus found there were some unexpected changes to his voice.

In my introduction to the warden at Johnson Prison, he told me there were a few special rules that needed to be followed. Warden Smith gave me the basic rules, but I told him that, since this was a death penalty state, I would like to work death row when he thought I was ready.

"So, Mike, you want to deal with the walking dead?"

"Well, I prefer to call them the condemned inmates living here."

"We will see how things go, and if I decide you're ready we'll talk."

"Thank you, Warden Smith."

As I left the warden's office on that first day, some questions were already popping up about some of his rules, like "Don't ask too many questions concerning the execution chamber" and "Don't push to become a death-row guard." To me these didn't make any sense, but I figured that for now I would follow the warden's unique set of rules.

On my first day I received a special assignment, to help clean up the execution chamber. The guard who I was working with, Davis, smiled at me and shook his head as we went to the chamber.

"The warden must have taken a real liking to you to let you into the chamber, even just to clean it up."

"I don't see any big deal about it. It's just another part of my job."

"Well, Mike, when you get inside we'll see if you still feel that way. Just remember, no questions!"

As we entered the chamber and turned on the light, I saw an unusual six-foot-by-six-foot room. And it was fully soundproofed.

There was no viewing room for the victims' convicts' families. I saw no equipment for execution in any way except a lone chair with heavy brown leather straps for the inmate's body, arms, and legs. As we prepared the chamber, I noticed a few stains on the floor, which we had to scrub to get clean. I was about to ask Davis a question when he saw my lips move and he shook his head to be quiet.

Davis and I finished and were leaving the chamber as I started to ask a few questions. "That is the most unusual execution chamber I have ever seen, Davis."

"Mike, didn't Warden Smith go over the special rules with you today?"

"Well, yes, he did, but I don't see what the big deal is. I'm just curious."

"If you're not careful you're going to curious yourself right out of your first guard job or worse. There are things that you just shouldn't ask about, and this is one of them."

With that, Davis walked quickly away from me, glancing over his shoulder at me like I had some sort of disease. I finished my first day at Johnson Prison with many questions that, if I believed Davis, it would be better I didn't ask.

The next day I was called to the warden's office, and while waiting I heard a quiet little voice speak my name. "Mike, the warden is ready for you."

That was my first meeting with Syrus Gupp. The funny thing was that I seemed to hear the voice, not so much with my ears as inside my head.

"Mike, I got a disturbing report about you asking questions about our execution chamber. I trusted you. That's why I put you on chamber cleanup on your first day. Didn't you understand the special rules I wanted observed?"

"Warden Smith, I know the rules you outlined in our meeting yesterday, but I don't fully understand their reason, and I guess my curiosity got the better of me."

"You have the potential to be a top guard in this prison, but too much curiosity killed the cat. You're dismissed, Mike, and please fucking adhere to my rules, to the letter!"

I left the warden's office humbled by the fact that I had been told off by the warden on my second day and ratted out by Davis in the first place. Who the hell did he think he was? He had only been here six months before me.

After that, things sort of cooled off between me and the rest of the prison staff, especially Davis. I went to check my watch schedule and start my rounds. Since most of the prison staff barely spoke two words to me, I talked with the inmates on my rounds, everyone from drug dealers to killers. Usually it was very casual conversation. Most didn't have regular visitors, so when someone new was around the opportunity to get fresh news was very important. I think that just talking to someone about anything was what was important.

As I was making my rounds, I saw Syrus Gupp walking alone down the cell block. I also noticed that the talking in the cells all stopped, and any inmates in the hallway crossed so they were as far away from Mr. Gupp as the walls would allow. Mr. Gupp seemed to have a very satisfied little smirk on his face as he looked over the inmates and how they behaved around him. What could this average-size humble desk clerk be a part of that made the inmates so nervous?

"Good day, Mike, how are you this nice sunny day?"

"Just fine, Mr. Gupp. Do you often roam the cell blocks alone?"

"I have nothing to fear from the men in this prison." He smiled.

As I walked farther along the cell block, one of the inmates motioned me over. "Officer, are you friends with Mr. Gupp?"

"My name's Mike, and no, not yet. I've only been here three days, but he's kind of an unusual guy, I think. Why?"

"My name is Jim, and I've been here for five years of a ten-year drug-dealing sentence. Mr. Gupp isn't the type of person you want to make friends with."

"What do you mean? He seems harmless."

"Do you know what the inmates here have nicknamed Mr. Gupp? The singer."

"What the hell does that mean?"

Just then Davis came walking around the corner, eyeing us both.

"Mike, you better get your rounds done as soon as possible. There was a schedule change. You're on yard detail this afternoon."

"Thanks, Davis, for letting me know."

"See me later if you want to talk more about Mr. Gupp, Mike," said Jim.

"Okay."

Duty in the yard was routine, and nothing happened until we started moving the inmates back inside. Suddenly a huge guy came up behind one of the inmates and stabbed him fifteen times with a shank. Blood was everywhere. The prisoners swarmed the scene, like a school yard fight rather than the death of a person. Yes, even though they were inmates, they were still people. By the time the inmates got herded into their cells and we got to the murderer and victim, it was no use. The victim was dead, and the big guy who murdered him was already on death row for murder. The murderer's name was Albert. As I turned the victim on his back to see who had died, my mouth opened in shock. As I stared at Albert, he started laughing out loud. I had just been talking to this inmate an hour ago. It was Jim.

Davis came up to me and helped me up.

"How does this happen so quickly, Davis? I was just talking to that inmate this morning."

"In here people are killed for the smallest things—to get at an inmate's stash of food or shoes, or maybe someone put a hit out on him."

"You're kidding, a hit?"

"You bet. For a carton of cigarettes anyone could be killed in here."

As we cleared the yard, I tried to clear my head and think about Jim's last words to me and what Davis had said. What kind of hell had I been dropped into? As I made my last rounds before I went home, no one spoke to me at all, even my regulars. I walked up to the common area and found a folded piece of paper with my name on it. When I read it I shivered. It said that talking too much was dangerous and to ask Jim. It wasn't signed. I was making progress! After three days I had been ratted out by another guard, told off by the warden, and had my first death threat! I was really climbing the ladder of success in my prison career!

The next day I reported the threatening letter to the warden, who shrugged it off as inmates jerking my chain and trying to shake up the new guy. Then he dismissed me.

I saw Davis at lunch the next day.

"Mind if I join you?"

"Not at all, Mike."

"Have you ever gotten death threats here?"

"Are you serious? No, never. Haven't even drawn my gun."

"Well, I just got my first death threat, and it scared the shit out of me."

I passed the letter to Davis, who looked pale after reading it. "Mike, I hate to say it, but I think someone is sending you a message. Jim's death must have been a hit."

"But what do I do? I like it here. It's interesting."

"I know a couple of inmates who know everything about this place and its skeletons. Maybe I can hook you up before you get killed by asking your dumb-ass questions."

Davis and I parted company with his promise that he would be in touch with me.

My sleep was about as restful as my next day at work, considering everything that had happened. As Davis and I ate lunch, he whispered that one of the older inmates was willing to bring me up to speed on how things worked in this prison so I didn't get killed by asking all my stupid questions. I was to meet him in an isolation cell at 9:00 p.m. Davis walked me to the meeting.

"After this talk you'll see why I had to report your questions. It was nothing against you, Mike, but more along the lines of self-preservation."

"Okay, I hope it's clearer to me after this meeting."

I walked into the isolation cell, and there sat an older inmate of about fifty. His gray hair was long but well groomed, and he smiled at me.

"Hello, my name is Mike, and I have a lot of questions about this prison."

"My name is John, and I'm in here for life because of a murder I did for revenge. I'm telling you this so you know that I am not trying to gain favor with you. What would you like to know first?"

"Well, what is the reason they nicknamed Mr. Gupp 'the singer' and why all the unusual rules about the execution chamber and asking questions?"

"All of that is tied together. First, the scars on Mr. Gupp's neck are from operations to save his voice and life when he was in an accident as a teenager. But it left Gupp with an interesting side effect. By singing certain notes, his vocal cords turn into lethal weapons, emitting ultrasonic waves that can sever the spinal cord and turn the brain to mush!"

"You have to be kidding, John. That sounds like science fiction!"

"You noticed the stains in the execution chamber, didn't you? It's like that after each execution. Also, it costs a lot of money to execute an inmate, and it's all paid for by the state. Since Gupp arrived, we haven't had an execution in the standard way in ten years, yet the warden keeps filing the execution orders and the money goes into the warden's and Gupp's pocket. In return, they pay off certain people to dispose of the bodies and write death certificates."

"This is so outrageous. How could this have kept going on without anyone saying anything?"

"First, Mike, you may want to check out cell 000 in the basement. It's used for storage. You may find it interesting. Next, and maybe most importantly, the inmate Jim who was killed was killed to send a message to you and other inmates about talking too much. That's why your friend Davis had to report you if anybody overheard you asking questions about the executions or the chamber. Let's just say in this prison people have disappeared for less—both inmates and staff."

I was silent for some time, and John just watched me as I tried to get my head around the fantastic story I had just been told.

"Thank you, John, for answering some of my biggest questions."

"That's okay, but we can't talk again. It would be too dangerous for me and you, so please just watch your back so you don't end up like Jim."

As I left the cell and walked with Davis, we were quiet all the way back to the ready room where we started and finished our shifts each day. Driving home, everything I had learned was rolling over in my head. I would have to do a lot of thinking over the next week to make any decisions. After a week I decided that I would try to help report the happenings at this prison, but I would have to wait till I had seen a real execution—Warden Smith style—before I could act. In the meantime I managed to check out the cell 000 they used for storage. I found it was used for storage, but half of it was covered with tarps. Under the tarps were all of the normal execution equipment, the electric chair, and all the equipment for lethal injections.

I decided to just keep to my own business and daily routine at the prison, keeping my nose clean. Maybe the warden would see fit to put me on the next execution detail. My chance came about a month later. When I got to the ready room and checked my schedule, I was on execution detail at the end of the week.

"Looks like you're moving up in the world for the warden to put you on execution detail this soon."

"Yeah, Davis, I guess he has taken a real shine to me."

When Friday came, the detail assembled outside the death chamber. The warden told us that the inmate had had a life sentence that the governor recently changed to the death penalty. The detail consisted of the warden, Mr. Gupp, Davis, and myself. We entered the chamber, and Davis looked back at me. I was the last to enter. The person being executed was John, who had clued me in on the inner workings of the prison. When our eyes met, he smiled a thin smile and his eyes watered just a bit. His arms and legs were strapped to the chair in the center of the room, and as I looked around the people in the room, both the warden and Mr. Gupp had knowing smirks on their faces. How I wanted to lash out and knock those stupid smiles off their faces, along with a couple of teeth down their throat with the help of my nightstick! I didn't dare let my emotions show on my face. John motioned me over to him.

"Warden, is it okay to approach the inmate?"

"Sure, it seems he wants to talk to you for a moment."

I moved close to John.

"They found out I talked to you, Mike. I think Gupp threatened your friend Davis to expose me."

"What can I do?"

"Remember everything, and don't forget me."

"I will never forget you, and I will get them!"

John shook my hand as best he could. Then the warden herded us all out of the chamber, except Mr. Gupp. After fifteen minutes, the door to the chamber opened and we saw that John was dead, blood and tissue leaking from his ears and nose.

"Now you're one of us, Mike, and as such you will find a little extra in your pay this week for serving on the execution detail."

Fuck that rat bastard warden, thinking he could buy me off with his scam on executions! I took the money and logged it, along with dates and who was executed, into an accounting book at home. I was going to nail these bastards.

The next day I contacted a friend of mine at the state attorney general's office. We met at a motel and talked. He had a hard time believing what I told him until I played a tape for him. I had been making tapes since Jim was murdered to protect myself. My friend called me later, and on the next day an inmate was executed, they would storm the prison and take the warden and Gupp into custody. The next execution wasn't scheduled for two weeks, and I informed my friend. On that occasion it was perfect, I thought, because the people who were writing the death certificates would also be at the prison. The warden had already filled out the execution papers, so he would be reimbursed by the state. Once again we were all on execution detail, but after ten minutes we heard excited voices coming from the center of the prison. As Gupp exited the chamber, smiling state cops came down the hallway. Both Warden Smith and Gupp took off running in the opposite direction to the cat calls from the inmates who saw what was happening.

"Mike, is this what you where askedto do?," Davis asked.

"Yes, Davis, it has to stop right now!"

Both the warden and Gupp heard Davis and me and stopped and turned for a moment.

"You stupid asshole, Mike!"

"Not as stupid as you, Warden!"

"Gupp, kill him in your own special way!"

Gupp smiled and started to sing his song of death, the notes becoming higher and more shrill. I screamed for everyone to cover their ears as best they could if they didn't want to die. The vocal cords on Gupp's neck stood out like thick bands, and we all had tears in our eyes from the sinus pain. I had to stop Gupp. I threw my nightstick as hard as I could toward his neck, making it spin fast. It struck Gupp across the throat, sending a gushing flood of blood out of his mouth and making him collapse. As I walked up to Gupp, he was dying.

"Mike, I'm not sorry for what I did. I was just using my special talents and ridding the world of its human garbage."

"I hope you include yourself in that category, Gupp."

I walked away in the direction of the warden, and as I turned the corner I saw a special sight: the warden being held against the cell bars by inmates as the state cops took him into custody.

"Arrest those guards there. They were part of it."

Just then my friend with the state arrived. "No, these guards are helping me with this sting. As I remember, Mike here has some tapes for us with evidence to be used at trial. Are there very many tapes, Mike?"

"About thirty-seven or so since an inmate named Jim was murdered here to send me a message."

The warden's face went white and red with rage as the state cops dragged him away. Both Davis and I got off as free as could be for turning in evidence, and Syrus Gupp's body was donated to a medical college to study his unique vocal cords.

THE UNKNOWN FACTOR

The driver had been putting in ten-hour days all week at the animal research lab. He was dead tired and almost falling asleep at the wheel on this last run of the day. He was sorry the animals had to be destroyed, but considering the experiments done on them with chemicals and genetic engineering, scientists couldn't chance any of the animals getting free. As the driver made his way into Clackamas County, he dozed off while going around a bend. He was in a coma for three days, but by the time he came out of the coma the animals that hadn't been killed in the crash or died soon after had wandered off into the lush forest full of food choices.

Five Years Later

The morning was brisk, and Linda was taking a long walk through the many acres of forest that she and her husband had bought so many years ago. Linda enjoyed strolling through the old logging roads and trails, collecting animal teeth and sometimes, if she was lucky, an animal skull. Besides, she felt she needed the exercise even though her friends didn't think so.

When Linda returned from her walk, her husband informed her that another unusual animal kill had occurred and that it was finally being picked up in the papers. Linda read the article: MYSTERIOUS ANIMAL KILLS TURNING UP THROUGHOUT EAGLE CREEK AND ESTACADA AREAS. LOCAL POLICE ARE ASKING FOR THE PUBLIC'S HELP. IF YOU SEE ANYTHING UNUSUAL, PLEASE CALL THE LOCAL POLICE.

Linda started wondering if any of the experimental animals could have survived this long. After all, everyone had heard about the crash, but nobody thought any of the escaped animals could have survived more than a couple of days—at least that's what they were telling the public.

Then one day Linda's friend across the way delivered some disturbing news. It seemed a mutual friend surprised an animal, attacking one of his steers. It had done so much damage to the steer that it had to be put down, and there wasn't much left of the mystery animal either. It seemed their friend got a bit excited and shot the thing so many times it almost disintegrated the animal, so identification was useless except that it left the same type of wounds on the steer that the mystery animal kills had.

Forensic biologist Norman Jacks was working patiently with the remains of the steer he had received. He made molds of tooth and bite impressions. He also collected saliva for DNA typing.

"How's it going, Norman?" asked Norman's friend Diane.

"It would have been a lot better if that guy with the steer hadn't gone off and declared World War III on this unusual critter."

Diane laughed. "Some of the people out in that area are trigger-happy."

"Diane, could you take a look at this impression of the wound I recently made? Maybe I've just been staring at it too long, but in the wound do you see anything unusual?"

Diane saw under magnification what Norman was talking about, a set of double teeth, leaving impressions like there had been two rows of teeth.

"Norman, this isn't possible. The only animal that even looks similar to this is the bite pattern of a shark."

After the steer attack, the police put out a warning to everyone who had any type of livestock or pets that they may be targets of this new animal roaming locally and to beware. Linda was very concenned, because their family had a few horses and a one-acre pond with nice-size fish.

 110

Back at the police station, the police chief, Dale Meers, was talking with his deputies. "Everyone, we are under the gun. So as to not panic people, we have set up a hotline for tips about the animal killings and to handle questions. We will not be spreading rumors about our investigation, not with our families or friends outside this office. Also, we deal in straight facts, nothing else. We may get visitors from the state forensic lab if we can find hard evidence, so treat each scene as a crime scene."

Linda was walking the next morning, a bit worried because of the latest developments, but the air smelled so good in the forest, the moist rich smell of the earth, and all the different animal noises as the forest woke up. She knew most of the sounds of the animals after the years she had lived in the area. Suddenly she heard a muffled grunting noise and running feet. Then an animal screamed, as if being caught in the jaws of a predator. This sound made the hair on the back of Linda's neck stand on end. Linda felt that she had walked enough for this morning and headed back home. All the way she had to keep telling herself that it was just an everyday animal she had heard grabbing its morning meal and not some genetically altered refugee from some science lab. If only Linda had turned around or glanced behind her as she got home she would have jumped. A large pair of glowing red eyes could be seen following her along the path she had taken. Wild animals have glowing yellow eyes when light reflects in them. The only light available was the morning light, and it was not red.

When Linda came inside later that day from feeding the horses, she heard her husband call her over near the path she had been walking that morning. They both looked at the soft ground next to the path. Footprints were obvious, but these prints didn't look like any predator they had ever seen around their home, and the tracks went right up to their house, circled it, and then went back into the woods. Linda's husband made a call to Officer Dale Meer, who was also a friend and fishing buddy. After hearing what his friend had to say, Dale called the state forensics lab and took some of his men out there.

Linda and her husband, Jeff, had never been in the middle of an investigation of any sort, but the disruption was unbelievable. There were no sirens or lights, but there were several vehicles with portable labs. Both Linda and Jeff were introduced to Diane and Norman from the state forensics lab.

"When you went for your walk this morning, did you notice anything unusual?" Norman asked Linda.

Linda paused a moment, thinking back to the odd sound she had heard and how to describe it to Norman. "I heard an unusual animal sound this morning that I had never heard, and I couldn't recognize the animal it came from. You have to understand I can identify most animal sounds from living here for so many years."

"Can you describe it to us?" Diane asked.

"I can try. It was very guttural, and it sounded like one animal pouncing on another, and there was a heaviness to its stride. When it ran I could hear its feet pounding the earth. The sound the animal made was bloodcurdling. I've never heard a sound like that from a dying animal before."

As the troopers made plaster castings of footprints and looked for bits of hair in the bushes, a couple of troopers went with Norman and Diane to backtrack to see if they could find where the mystery animal had made its kill. They had searched about a mile into the woods when they came to a clearing about ten feet in diameter. There was a mangled mass of hide and flesh in the center, blood everywhere, and an ear from a good-size doe. But the volume of meat and hide didn't match the probable size of the doe. Most of the animal had been eaten right on the spot, which shocked both Norman and Diane. They took samples for their lab and advised Linda and Jeff that maybe morning walks should be put on hold until they caught this animal. An animal with such a hunger would be very dangerous.

When Diane and Norman got the evidence back to their lab, the plaster casts of the tracks got their first attention. This animal had six toes spread evenly with long hooked claws at the end of each toe. By the indentations in the soil, they estimated each claw was three and a half inches long and very likely razor sharp. Also, the paw was massive, ten inches across. It was easy to see how an animal equipped like this could take down larger animals quickly. There had been very little evidence of animal hairs around the site, but those that were found were all identified as common animals, with the exception of three hairs. These hairs were six inches long, black, and almost silky in texture. But the most important thing about the hairs was that they had roots attached, which meant that they had a possible DNA sample of the new animal. Norman and Diane started the analysis right away.

Linda was sitting in her home, nervous as could be with all that had been going on the past few days. Jeff noticed this and suggested that maybe working in their garden in the cool evening air would calm her down just before night fell. That sounded like a good idea, and as Linda picked up a few tools and headed to the garden, she realized she was already relaxing. As Linda worked, she noticed the many animal sounds around her, mostly birds, but once in a while she heard larger animals like deer, raccoons, and squirrels moving through the forest. Linda looked up, casually wiping the sweat from her brow and looking at the sunset. She realized the animals had stopped making any type of sounds. A cold sweat and goose flesh broke out on Linda's arms, and her sense of calm had started to climb into the realm of fear. Linda stood slowly and intended to walk calmly back to the house, but as soon as she stood something behind her emitted a low guttural growl. Linda froze. Whatever it was didn't sound like it was big but rather low to the ground, maybe about three feet. Linda realized she was going to have to make a stand if she didn't want to be attacked. She had been grasping a shovel when she stood up for support, its broad pointed metal front a very good weapon. If she could just connect with one solid blow she would have a chance to get back to her home and Jeff. Linda firmly grasped the shovel handle and heard the mystery animal growl again. She fixed in her mind about where the head would be and swung the shovel as hard as she could.

As she turned to swing the shovel, Linda got a glimpse of the animal, as horrifying a sight as she had ever thought she would see: red eyes, long silky black fur, long claws, muscular body, and a snarling mouth full of pointed razor-sharp teeth. She didn't need to correct her aim. The broad side of the shovel caught the animal between the nose and eye. Blood flew from the animal's mouth, and a shriek of surprise came from this ugly animal, causing Linda to run to her house and the animal to head into the forest, still crying out. As she slammed the door shut, she started to cry and told Jeff the whole story. Jeff just held her until she calmed down. Then he called Officer Dale Meer and relayed the whole story. Officer Meer would be out the next morning with a forensics team.

Officer Meer and his team started searching the area by the garden where Linda had her encounter, but for the longest time nothing could be found. Then a deputy called the forensics team over to photograph and collect one specimen, a tooth with twin points and long roots.

"Looks like your wife connected pretty well with that shovel, Jeff. Seems we found one of the teeth she knocked out of its mouth."

When they showed the tooth to Jeff and Linda, they couldn't believe how small it was yet how deadly it looked, with its twin points of cutting edges.

Norman and Diane looked over the tooth and spoke to Jeff and Linda. "Do you have any guns in the house?" asked Norman.

"No, not a one. Why do you ask?" asked Jeff.

"Well, the animal that this tooth came from was a smaller version of what attacked your friend's steer, and if the full-size version came about you would need a gun, especially since you hurt one of the younger ones," Diane stated.

"Jeff, I can loan you my elk rifle and some ammo."

"Thanks, Dale, I think I'll take you up on that."

Once everybody had cleared out from Jeff and Linda's and Jeff had Dale's rifle, a small sense of security started to creep back into their lives.

Back at the forensics lab, Diane and Norman examined the tooth. The DNA examination told them only that this was a genetically engineered animal; however, the tooth told them much about the killing ability of the creature. First, a full-size adult capable of attacking a steer must weigh in at around five hundred to six hundred pounds and be incredibly strong.

"Norman, I hope Linda's husband got that elk rifle. He may need it to deal with the other adult if it comes calling," Diane said.

It had been several days since the police had been there and found the tooth. There hadn't been any more weird animal noises or encounters, and as a matter of fact, the mysterious animal killings had slowed way down.

Then as Linda and Jeff were relaxing one evening, a huge crash startled them. It came from their deck.

"Jeff, what the hell was that?"

"I don't know. Let me take a look."

As Jeff looked out the window, a large lump lay in the middle of their deck, and thirty yards away a massive animal sat in their yard, staring at their home, its red eyes glowing. The thing on the deck was the animal that Linda had encountered a few days ago, the side of its face badly damaged. Jeff went to get the elk rifle as Linda watched out the windows.

"Jeff, that thing is charging the front of our house."

Suddenly there was a loud crash and splintering deck railing as the animal turned to charge again.

"I'm hurrying."

Jeff loaded the rifle as fast as he could and came downstairs. Linda had tipped over a sofa for protection. Jeff came downstairs just in time to see this hulk of an animal take the siding off an area of his house. With the last charge, the picture window in the front had shattered. There was nothing between the animal and Jeff and Linda. As the animal charged, its nostrils flared, Jeff brought the rifle up and fired every round into the animal's chest. The animal was charging at full speed and probably died on its feet, but its momentum carried it into Jeff and Linda's living room.

After they called the police, who hauled away the animal, it was determined that it was the female of the mating pair. The forensics people theorized that when Linda struck the younger animal, it probably died sometime later, with the female coming back to avenge her young's untimely death.

"Well, Jeff, guess you won't be needing my rifle anymore."

"No, Dale, I'm just glad it's all over with so we can get back to a normal life."

Deep in the hills around Estacada there are many caves used by bears, cougars, and other animals for homes. In one of them the three occupants wait for their parents and other sibling to return as they peer out at the world with fire-red eyes!

TUMBLEWEEDS REVENGE

His name was Errol Mienum, and because of his track record of numerous acts of violence since he was fifteen, he earned the nickname Evil Errol. Among Errol's many interests were rape, murder, being an escape artist, and recently a Satan worshipper. Errol was serving a life sentence in a prison in the desolate area of eastern Oregon, where escape just meant death by Mother Nature instead of in prison. Errol had been suffering from being in prison so long, twenty of his thirty-five years, and had become more agitated and abusive to the prison staff and other prisoners. One day he caught a break. All inmates were told that, if they were on their best behavior, they would be considered for a work-release program at the end of the week. Errol needed to get out, even if it was only for a few hours. He prayed to Satan. Errol actually indulged in many strange cult beliefs, but Satanism was the one he really enjoyed. He was a model prisoner all week and even helped out several times to diffuse tense situations. The guards couldn't believe it and, against their better judgment, okayed Errol for the work-release program. It was announced to the general prison population that the work release would be land reclamation at the old Sloth Farm, an area that had gone to barren fields as far as the eye could see. They were tearing the main place down, it turned out.

When they arrived in the prison bus, it was already ninety degrees at ten in the morning. As the inmates started to tear the main building down, the two lonely guards that were watching them grew bored. The work didn't get done till eight at night, and as Errol sat in the cooling evening, skin sticking to the vinyl-covered bus seats, he wished for some dark intervention to allow him to escape.

Errol fell asleep and dreamed of only a voice from the dark saying over and over, "Be ready, be ready."

Suddenly Errol found himself tumbling through the bus along with the other inmates, some of whom were screaming. When Errol came to a stop, he got up. Some of the riders of the bus were moaning and bleeding. Others were silent, eyes wide open, staring into space, their broken dead bodies icy cold.

Errol removed himself and started walking toward the Columbia River in hopes of finding food and water, all the while thinking, *This is my chance!*

Mike Shear arrived at the office that morning to a group of messages he didn't want, including more livestock mutilations and a potential prison escape.

"Holy crap, we have twenty-six prisoners from the local prison who did not return from their work-release program. That's all we need, prisoners roaming the area!"

Errol was close to death due to dehydration and exposure. He was also getting delusional. He fell to his knees and asked Satan how he could let this happen to him after all the excellent evil he had done. Suddenly tumbleweeds started to press and gather around Errol as the wind picked up.

"Please allow me to live on somehow. I will give you my soul!"

Suddenly the tumbleweeds not only pressed into Errol but their thorns started ripping at his flesh. Errol heard a deep dark voice: "Your evil will live on through the tumbleweeds, Errol. Ha ha ha!"

"But that's not what I meant!" Errol heard the laughter in his ears till he died.

Mike took a few deputies out to the work-release site. About halfway there they got their first surprise. A truck hauling barrels of toxic waste had over turned into a ditch and spilled the contents of the barrels. The second surprise was about five miles farther when they came upon the overturned prison bus filled with dead bodies—except one: Errol's.

Errol had been a suspect in many crimes, including the one that had finally landed him in prison. One of Mike's deputies came in that afternoon.

"Mike, we found something out about five miles from here that you should look at."

Mike rode out with his deputy and found a large pile of tumbleweeds. In the center were the remains of a prison uniform and the remains of Errol Mienum. He was virtually ripped apart. If that wasn't strange enough, written in the dirt by Errol's finger were the words MY EVIL WILL LIVE ON THROUGH THESE TUMBLEWEEDS!

At the time Mike just took it as the words of a lunatic dying from exposure.

Steve Johnson was getting ready to tend his farm animals early in the morning when he heard a loud commotion coming from the barn. Steve ran to the barn, thinking a coyote or wolf had gotten into it. As he threw open the barn door, his mouth fell open. All his animals were dead, ripped apart, and somehow tumbleweeds were everywhere in the barn. They must have come through the hay loft, he thought. As Steve looked for the culprit who murdered his livestock, he stepped slowly, heard a low rustling behind him, and turned. The pathway out of the barn was blocked by tumbleweeds, their long thorns stained dark with blood. Before Steve could react, the tumbleweeds launched themselves at Steve, devouring him in the same way as his livestock, and all the while a man's voice kept laughing in his ear.

Stan Billings came rushing into the sheriff's office. "Mike, I was just over to Steve Johnson's place. We were supposed to go fishing. He's been murdered!"

Mike and a couple of deputies went out to Steve's. It was the most horrible thing they had seen. One of the deputies puked hard. Mike was thinking how this looked strangely like how Errol had died, but no tumbleweeds were around. Buts they were leaving Mike noticed a piece of tumbleweed with longer-than-normal thorns stained with blood. He bagged the piece as evidence and left.

Back at the office Mike had the lab test the piece of tumbleweed. It had both animal and human blood on it.

"Do you guys think the animal cases we've had could be tied in with the Johnson murder?"

"We don't know. It sounds a little far-fetched, doesn't it?"

"Well, guys, do you remember the overturned truck hauling the toxic waste? There were traces of that waste in the piece of tumbleweed I had the lab test for blood."

The faces in the sheriff's office looked shocked.

"How are we going to fight tumbleweeds that have a mind of their own?" one deputy asked.

"That I haven't figured out yet, but we had better figure it out in a hurry before more people are killed," Mike said with a lot of worry in his voice.

Helen had lived in her home for thirty years and had electricity only to her home, not her barn. One night she heard a big commotion out in her barn. As she grabbed a lantern she ran as fast as she could to the barn. The animals were in a frenzy, crying out. As Helen threw open the barn door, she gasped as she saw one of her cows covered in tumbleweeds as it was being ripped apart. Helen screamed and hurled the lantern at the floor nearest the tumbleweeds. The lantern smashed and lit the tumbleweeds on fire. As she herded the animals that were still alive out of the barn, the flames grew larger and a wind came up. It seemed to be screaming as the tumbleweeds burned. Helen had never seen tumbleweeds burn with such ferocity and huge flames before, and the heat they gave off made her take her animals into her home with her.

"Sheriff, this is Helen Aets. I need your help. Something strange has happened that I think you should take a look at."

"Okay, Helen, we will be right out," Mike told her.

Mike had been on his way home when the call came in. It seemed with this job he was always putting in overtime. When Mike arrived at Helen's place he saw the burned remains of the barn, and as Helen opened the door to answer Mike's knock he saw her remaining animals inside with her. Mike took Helen aside as his deputies looked over the burned barn for clues.

"Helen, what happened here, and why are your animals in your home?"

"Mike, if I tell you the truth you might lock me up in the loony bin."

"Just tell me what happened. You've known me since I was a kid. Trust me."

So Helen relayed her story to Mike, and she was surprised at how unshocked and attentive he was. Lately Mike was starting to get used to weird happenings in their area.

"Helen, how did your barn start burning?"

"When I saw what was happening it scared me, so the only thing I could think of was to burn those tumbleweeds and save my other animals."

"Don't worry about your barn. I know some guys who owe me a favor. We can have a pole barn up for you today and a more permanent structure later, okay?"

"Thank you, that would be great."

One of the deputies brought some burned tumbleweed to Mike. "Thought you would want to see this, Mike."

Mike looked at the piece of tumbleweed. "So it's burned. What's your point, Deputy?"

"It's not just burned. If you look along the branches they're withered like they died."

Mike smiled. "So they are."

Mike got together with his deputies and mapped out where all the tumbleweed attacks had occurred. It turned out that they were all equidistant from where Evil Errol's body was found. Mike and some of his deputies decided to take a trip during the day back out to where they found Errol's body. When they got out there they were shocked by what they saw, so much so that they took pictures for evidence. It seemed that the whole area where Errol died was drawing tumbleweeds to it by the hundreds. And although there was no wind on this day, they seemed to be rustling. Quietly Mike and his men left to return to the office and form a plan. As the deputies worked on their job preparations for the next day, they all wondered what would happen.

Mike assembled everyone and explained what they would do. "We are going to use a combination of flamethrowers and hazardous chemical retardants to kill these things off. The tanks will combine the two chemicals and hopefully burn the hell out of them."

The deputies and Mike went to the area where they hoped to kill the tumbleweeds off, parking a quarter of a mile away. The men stayed below the ridge of the area that held the tumbleweeds until they were all in place, ringing the area.

On Mike's order they opened fire, releasing the chemical flame mixture on the tumbleweeds. Suddenly the tumbleweeds came to life, creating a wall. The wind started to come up and like a living animal on fire the wind shreiked a blood curdling scream.

"Don't let any of them attack you, men!" Mike yelled above the burning tumbleweeds.

More and more of the tumbleweeds were throwing themselves at the deputies, and Mike realized that the screaming wind sounded very familiar. It sounded like Evil Errol's voice.

"No, you can't destroy my evil, Sheriff. No!"

Mike just smiled as his men used the flamethrowers until every one of them was empty, even burning the ashes.

Mike was happy that they all got away with only some minor injuries, but to this day when Mike dreams he hears Errol's voice threatening to come back, and Mike wonders, *Did we get all of the tumbleweeds?*

CPSIA information can be obtained at www.ICGtesting.com
Printed in the USA
LVOW090244120112

263438LV00005B/48/P